I See You:

ICU

Pamela Roland

Also by Pamela Roland

What to Expect While in Drud & Alcohol Detox

I Hear You

Pamela Roland

I See You:

ICU

ISBN: 978-0-578-72977-0

Special thanks to the editing assistance of Write Your Best Book.

Dedicated to my sons Scott, Tony, and Greg

and to my grandson, Brady, the apple of my eye.

Chapter 1

In 1805, the Louisiana Purchase two years prior, was still fresh on the locals' minds, and

all were happy about President Jefferson's decision to purchase the land from France, even

though many opposed him. Most of the newly established Louisianans still felt a connection to

Napoleon but reveled in their newfound independence.

The bayou of Louisiana was steamy-hot on a summer afternoon, and the smell of salt and fish filled the air as the seaweed bobbed up and down in the waves. Pelicans' calls filled the windy air as shrimp boats sailed along the horizon with nets straining against the pressure of their catch, with a faint song of an akonting in the distance, when the wind was right. Waves gently slapped on the shore, mimicking a percussion background as the seagulls sang.

Being in love at the tender age of seventeen, Francesca appreciated these sights and sounds more than most as her long red hair blew in the breeze. The sunshine reflected off her flawless complexion and green eyes. Although all her twenty-six dates with Philip had been chaperoned, her parents were eager to marry Francesca off. Although Francesca knew their eagerness was for financial reasons, she was truly in love with Philip. She dreamed of his curling brown locks, and his deep brown eyes, while his strong arms made her feel safe when she was with him, and she knew his pouting lips had a familiar smile only meant for her.

Her parents, Marianna and Edward, had seven other daughters to feed and looked forward to the day of fewer people in their two-room house. She spent many hours talking with Philip on her front porch, and he would always bring her a bouquet of wildflowers tied with a simple string, and her mother always made tea for them and was happy to leave them unattended to talk. Francesca would place her flowers on the rustic dining table for all her family to enjoy, but she would always pull one small flower to lay next to her bed to smell all throughout her dreams at night. Her dreams always consisted of running through the fields with Philip and laughing.

Marianna and Edward also believed in educating women, and as an uneducated woman herself, Marianna pursued a scholarship for Francesca to the only school in the new world for girls past sixth grade. They also knew they could not afford to do this for each child, so they expected Francesca to pass-on her education to her younger siblings. She was happy to oblige and teaching them also helped her to become a better student. Each evening before bed, she would sit in front of the fire with all her siblings and individualize their studies according to their age. She always loved the science portions.

At school, she spent all her day studying and helping with the younger students. She carried a raw potato to school each day and placed it on the woodstove to bake throughout the morning. By lunch time, it was perfectly cooked and filled the classroom with a savory aroma. She always thought this was a nice treat, and she occasionally accompanied the potato with raw carrots as well, if her family's garden had some to spare.

That particular evening, after drying the last of the clay dinner plates, and picking a book to read to her sisters, Francesca saw a glimpse of Philip walking down the trail earlier than usual. Her mother gave a familiar nod toward the front door, giving Francesca permission to skip her nightly reading and sit with Philip. She was already in her rocking chair when Philip started up the three steps. She tried to hide her disappointment when she noticed he had no flowers in his hand.

Philip took Francesca's hand as he had done every evening for several months. He led her away from the porch and toward the open meadow. Francesca was afraid to ask what was wrong, and Philip continued his silence. Finally, when reaching the edge of the woods, he turned to Francesca and swallowed hard, as if to gather his courage. "Francesca, I have some terrible news," Philip whispered. They both stood quietly, as neither wanted to delve further into the conversation. Philip was the first to break the silence.

"My parents are making me move back to France where I was born. I did not know that they had planned this since my birth. They never told me." Philip's eyes teared up. "I begged them not to send me." One big tear ran down Francesca's face. She could not move. The fresh night air became a choking fog as her entire world seemed to be in question.

Finally, Francesca managed to eke out, "Why?" After more silence from Philip, she thought she must be in a bad dream. *How could she awaken herself from such a nightmare? Why won't he answer me? What do his parents have planned? How can I go on living?* "Can I go with you?" she asked plopping down into the grass. "I want to go with you. Take me with you. Marry me and take me with you." She stood again, pacing, and looking at Philip for answers. *Why wouldn't he answer?*

She lifted Phillip's chin with one finger and asked, "Why?" She saw his red and swollen eyes; he had obviously been crying for a long time. He kept his gaze toward the ground and could not look into her eyes. Her astonishment and sadness turned to fear. "What is it Philip?"

"I must go. There is no way out of this. I've tried." He sighed and looked sadly into her eyes. "I did not know, my darling. I did not know." He put his face into his hands, trying to hide his tears.

"You didn't know what Philip? Tell me, tell me now," Francesca's fear changed into anger and frustration, as she wiped away her tears. Pulling on his arm, she could not take this any longer. She wanted answers. "I need to know."

Philip looked down, took a deep breath, and said heavily," I am to marry my second-cousin. Both of our parents arranged this before we were even born. She lives in Europe." The words became reality as Philip raised his head and looked Francesca in the eye, and the words hit Francesca like a dagger in her heart. *How could this be?*

The trees and Spanish moss blowing in the wind, the sweet songs of the birds, and the smell of the honeysuckle, all shrunk into her tunnel vision of Philips eyes. This was not a bad dream; dreams do not hurt this much. Her muscles weakened as she saw his sorrow. She was rarely speechless but could not form a word.

Francesca felt her knees trembling and growing weak. Philip's handsome face began to seem fuzzy, and the trees spun in Francesca's peripheral vision, just before she lost consciousness and fell to the ground.

Her next sight was her father patting her cheek as she lay on her bed. She looked to the left and to the right, expecting to see Philip, but the only other person present was her mother with a glass of water. Her father informed her that Philip had left in tears after he carried her all the way back to the house, explained his situation, and kissed her on the forehead. Her parents felt helpless in what to do or say to their precious daughter to make her feel better. They simply hugged her in silence.

The next morning Philip was gone. His parents had taken him for their two-week-long carriage trip to escort him to the Georgia coast, where he was to catch a ship for France. Without warning or preparation, Francesca's world had crumbled. Her parents' words, her sisters' encouragement, or her Bible verses, could not pull Francesca out of her deep depression.

As the weeks and months passed, Francesca went through all her daily routines of chores, walking to her all-girls school the Catholic Ursuline Academy, staring at her textbooks, walking home from school, and picking at her uneaten dinner. The only time her eyes sparkled was at mail-delivery time at the local merchant on her days off school. Every day she would wait for a letter from Philip saying he had changed his mind and was coming home, and every day nothing came. She received no letters from Philip. Although she had always put others' needs and wants before her own, she had even stopped caring about others including her siblings. She stopped reading to them or teaching them all together.

After months of watching Francesca's depressed mood grow darker, and her studies decline, her teacher Mr. Verone, tried to console her after school one evening. Mr. Verone was a kind and caring teacher with a glowing smile that made people take a second look. His eyes were a vibrant green, and his thick, black hair shined in the numerous candle lights in the school. He had watched Francesca lose her will to participate, and perhaps her will to even live, more each day until she turned no homework in at all and never participated in class. Mr. Verone knew of the tragedy that happened to Francesca. He knew Francesca had not heard from Philip. Philip's parents had told Mr. Verone that Philip was enrolled in a university in France and scheduled to be married two weeks earlier, and their intention to combine and double the family's wealth. He sat on the school steps with Francesca and attempted to encourage and bring Francesca out of her depression, but Francesca only stared into the woods and down the path that led to her house.

There had been talk of Mr. Verone having a tragic loss in his past; perhaps a wife or child, but he had never spoken of it in the three straight years he had taught Francesca. He always had a stern and protective look to him, but with kind eyes. It was those kind eyes that led Francesca to trust him. Francesca felt that perhaps Mr. Verone might understand her pain and growing mistrust of men.

Finally putting an arm around Francesca, Mr. Verone wished her a good evening and a safe journey home. Francesca, stood slowly, and trudged toward the path in the woods. Mr. Verone watched her disappear into the trees. He always stayed in the school room long after all the students had left, and Francesca had never seen him anywhere but in the classroom.

Francesca passed the tree stump that she and Philip used to sit on. The wildflowers blew in the wind, whispering Philips name. The bluebirds chirped as they always did when she and Philip whistled to them. The Spanish moss rustled and reminded her of the day she and Philip played tag and he ran right into a mossy clump that covered his face. They laughed and laughed at the sight. Everything reminded Francesca of Philip. There was no escape, but the pain and sadness turned to feelings of anger and betrayal.

As she walked through the woods, she looked back several times. Why, she did not know; she felt like she was being watched. Whenever she looked back, she saw nothing but the darkening trail behind her. She did not hurry her pace from fear, and she did not care what happened to her anymore. Soon, she stopped looking back at all.

Moments later, a warm breeze passed by her ear like a hot breath. Francesca spun around only to find nothing there. A chill ran up her spine, and she stopped in her track's. After a moment, she took one more look behind her seeing nothing, then back toward her journey to her loneliness in a house full of people.

Without a sound, without warning, a dark figure stood right in front of her. This person did not say a word. Francesca could not breathe from fear. A long minute of silence and terror lingered between them, when the figure took a step forward; it was Mr. Verone.

"I'm sorry to startle you, my dear. I worried you were feeling too ill to make it home on your own," Mr. Verone said. Francesca let out a huge sigh and plopped onto a rock as fear and relief took her last bit of strength. Mr. Verone sat beside her and put his arm around her to comfort her. They sat for several minutes before either spoke.

"What can I do to help you my dear?" Mr. Verone whispered. "I know how you feel, for I too, have lost a dear love long, long ago." Francesca exploded in sobbing tears. There was no consoling her; she could not speak until she muttered the words, "I can't go on!" Mr. Verone did not speak; he only watched Francesca in silence.

The hand that was on Francesca's shoulder now caressed her back. Francesca finally felt a little comfort. She was oblivious to the other hand now on her right knee. Her teacher kissed her cheek and slid his hand under Francesca's dress. Francesca wriggled, giving Mr. Verone permission to continue. She was overwhelmed with the emotion.

Mr. Verone moved his lips around to meet Francesca's open and welcoming mouth. Their kiss was deep and passionate as they both moaned with delight. "I have a solution for your loss and can

make you want to live again. I know you don't want to go on,"
Patrick hissed.

Patrick's words made her realize she had lost control. "No!"
Was the only word she could muster. She had almost let this man
defile her innocence. She wriggled away, sat up, and told him to get
away.

When Francesca caught her breath, she looked up at the
moon. *Was this another dream?* It was so surreal. Mr. Verone stood
and looked down into Francesca's green eyes lit by the moon.
Francesca's emotions changed from lust to terror when seeing Mr.
Verone's stare. Her teacher's eyes changed from a look of care and
concern to moonlit sensuality and evil as he growled, "It's not your
fault my dear. Your only mistake was to trust men." He pinned her
down, ripped her skirt off, and entered her forcefully, as her screams
for help went unanswered. Her pleas were silenced as she felt Mr.
Verone's set of fangs as they sunk into her neck.

The chaos in the intensive care unit at Atlanta Southern Hospital was at its usual high level, when a loud alarm interrupted the constant chirps and beeps. This alarm meant someone's heart was approaching asystole cardiac arrest. As registered nurses and respiratory technicians ran to the room of Mr. Cleveland, he lay looking up at the ceiling, with his back arched up off the bed, yelling, "My back, my back! It's killing me!" Little did he know how correct he was. The heart monitor on the wall showed a large tombstone-looking pattern, as the RN, Barry, turned up the nitroglycerin drip. The other RN, Ruth, injected 5 milligrams of morphine into his intravenous line.

"Call a code, and make sure Dr. Philips knows her patient is circling the drain," Barry said to Ruth, without looking up or hesitating and while shuffling through the many intravenous lines, turning some drips up, turning others down, and hooking up the code cart monitor to the patient, who was still screaming in pain. "It's okay Mr. Cleveland; We're right here and going to make you more comfortable. I am going to guess your pain is a ten out of ten and that it would be a stupid question to ask. Dr. Philips is on her way – in fact, here she is now, and your family is right outside the door; I will let them in to visit you in a few minutes."

Both Barry and Ruth were relieved to see Dr. Francesca Philips as she strode into Mr. Cleveland's room. Neither knew her well, as she never seemed to open up to her coworkers, and neither would consider her a "friend", but both were glad to see she was the physician on duty. Ruth had seen many doctors in her years at the hospital, and she recognized Dr. Philips (Ruth could never call a doctor by their first name - not how she was trained) was one of the good ones: very capable, very skilled, and someone who knew how special and precious life was. Barry appreciated Francesca's confidence and the way she always seemed in control. He only called her by her first name after she prompted him; he respected the proper chain of command. Although she appeared to be even younger than he was, and even with his previous eight years working in a military war zone, she always gave Barry the feeling that she had experienced so much more than he had. He also noticed that while doctors and nurses all must be accustomed to the sight of blood, it always seemed that Francesca was almost thrilled by it, but Barry and Ruth never doubted that Dr. Philips would always put the best interest of the patients above any other consideration.

Francesca hurried to the monitor, ordered an amiodarone intravenous push, and to be followed by an amiodarone drip. Barry had the medication in his pocket, and immediately administered it; but it was too late. Mr. Cleveland's eyes roll back in his head; he collapsed on the bed and went into a ventricular tachycardia. Ruth said, "Dr. Levi, his family doctor, has asked that we continue to keep him a full code." With that statement, the sticky pads were applied to his chest, the joules were set at 150, Barry announced "clear," and Francesca pushed the defibrillator button.

"I don't care what Dr. Levi asks, if he does not ever come into this ICU to visit his patient, I will call the shots. Does his family know we are coding this lovely man?" Francesca asked as she watched Mr. Cleveland's back arch into a spastic contortion, and she re-evaluated the rhythm strip on the code cart. As Francesca ordered the RNs to push epinephrine intravenously and re-shock Mr. Cleveland, she took one step backwards, and into the hallway, and motioned for Mr. Cleveland's wife to come into the room. A look of disbelief overtook Mrs. Cleveland's face as she saw the brutal force of CPR now being thrust upon her husband. "Mrs. Cleveland," Francesca whispered, "I wanted you to see for yourself what state your husband has come to. I think it's fair that you get to see and decide for yourself if we should continue this process or stop and let your husband go."

Mrs. Cleveland stared at her husband as another round of jolts surged through his body and the ICU team treated his failing heart, as they had done thousands of times before on other patients. As Mrs. Cleveland's shaky voice broke through her surreal vision, she gasped, "Stop, please stop."

All activity ceased in the room. Only the slowing beeps of the machines could be heard. Francesca and Ruth stepped to Mrs. Cleveland and held her hand, as Barry detached the breathing tube, removed the defibrillator pads, and made Mr. Cleveland appear as if he was taking a nap. With her arm around Mrs. Cleveland's shoulders, Francesca softly spoke, "Mrs. Cleveland take all the time you need, we'll be right outside, and we'll do anything you wish."

With tears running down her cheeks, Mrs. Cleveland could not speak; she simply nodded as the team exited the room. The Cleveland's children and grandchildren slowly entered the room to hold Mr. Cleveland's hand as they heard the last bleeps on the machines and then a constant whistle of flat-lined asystole. Barry silenced all these alarms from his desk. Since she knew the registered nurses would handle all the post-mortem details, such as the coroner transportation, the funeral home, and all the paperwork to be signed by the family, she left the details in their capable hands, and saw no need to order an autopsy for this gentleman.

Francesca walked to the other end of the ICU, where another of her patients, Rose, was doing much better. Rose was sitting up, watching a late, late television talk show, and eating a light snack on her bedside table. She had a large bandage wrapped around her head, as she had mysteriously "*fallen*" down the stairs a few days earlier. Francesca knew this was not the true story, because when Rose spoke of her encounter, she looked down and to the right, which usually indicated a person is lying. Francesca knew Rose is right-handed, and that when right-handed people lie, their eyes often moved down and to the right.

The ICU room looked like all the others; large, glass doors made up the entire front wall, and opened to allow large beds with heavy life-supporting machinery access in and out. An overhead monitor displayed EKG rhythms, arterial waves, pulmonary-artery values, and frequent vital signs. Rose's overhead monitor had previously displayed her intracranial pressures. A small sink, hinged to the wall, opened like a door to reveal a seldom-used commode inside. A small television, attached by a brace, hung from the ceiling. Several intravenous pumps with varying sizes of fluid bags hung from the tall, metal poles, jumbled together near the head of the bed. Most of the intravenous lines threaded and juncture into one another before attaching to the central intravenous line taped to Rose's chest that went directly into her heart.

Francesca had seen abuse too many times and had seen the victims lie on behalf and defend their attackers, so she kept a watchful eye out for Rose's visitors. Francesca suspected a boyfriend, who had not yet visited Rose since her admission five days ago, at least not during her night shift. When Rose was admitted she was in a coma. She had a ventricular drain inserted through her skull to relieve the increasing pressure on her brain, which was removed yesterday due to her speedy improvement.

As Francesca entered the room, Rose turned the television volume down. Her right eye was swollen and black, but her smile let Francesca know that Rose would be okay. As Francesca flipped through her chart on her small laptop computer, she reviewed her labs, scanned over her latest brain CT, reviewed her vital signs, and made small talk with Rose. She knew questioning Rose would only make her more reclusive about a topic of her injury. "Rose," she chimed, "you have made a wonderful recovery and I'm proud of you."

"Thank you, Dr. Francesca, I couldn't have done it without you," Rose whispered in her scratchy voice resulting from the endotracheal tube removed yesterday. As they talked about Rose's plans when she would be sent home, Francesca checked the intravenous lines, the color of her urine in her Foley catheter, capillary refill in her toes, and scanned the room for flowers: more precisely, she was looking for a card on the flowers so she could read the name of the sender. Visitors were rare in the hospital at this late hour, but the ICU had visiting hours from four to five AM. When the only flowers in the room seemed to be from her mother, she squeezed Rose's hand, and went back to the dictation room to document today's progress.

Francesca entered all the events of Mr. Cleveland's earlier code, signed the death certificate, signed the autopsy waiver, and signed and witnessed the code-blue chart Ruth had completed and left for her in the electronic chart. Francesca saw that Barry had the death packet completed and signed by the family and had notified the local funeral home. A small smile crept over Francesca's face when she noticed the family had chosen Moore Funeral Home, as her dear friend, Patrick Moore, owned and ran the business.

Francesca stood to see if she could catch the driver of the hearse before they left with Mr. Cleveland's body. She knew Patrick often made the late-night body-pickups himself to save his employees from being awakened, and he also did not have to pay them overtime. When she entered the hallway of Mr. Cleveland's room, Patrick was just leaving with the covered body on a stretcher and heading for the elevator. They nodded a hello at each other, without saying a word, and Patrick gave Francesca a quick wink, and pushed the elevator button. No one noticed this subtle, unspoken communication. Francesca turned on her heel with a smile and headed back toward the dictation room.

As she walked past Rose's doorway, she noticed Rose had a visitor. She invented a reason to re-visit Rose, get closer, and check out the man sitting in the chair on the other side of her bed. He was tall, thin, had a scruffy beard, and shifty eyes. "Oh Dr. Francesca," Rose managed with her shaky voice, "meet my boyfriend, Bruce." Bruce rose from his chair and hurriedly walked toward the door and Francesca. Francesca did not budge.

"Nice to meet you," Bruce said as he turned sideways to edge by Francesca through the door, "I was just leaving." Still Francesca did not move; she kept her eyes on Rose, took a deep breath, smelling the man's scent. *Smells like boring and bland O negative*, she thought. As she finally let his pass, she saw a familiar, meek, smile as she had seen in so many other abused women.

When Rose said she would like to take a nap, rolled over toward the window, and pulled the covers up to her neck, Francesca knew this was the man who had beaten her with a hard object. She knew this was the man who had the nerve to return to his battered girlfriend with apologies and shallow kindness, just as most abusive men do.

Francesca turned and walked down the hall in the direction Bruce had headed. She could not see him but heard the elevator chime as the doors were closing. She knew he was headed to the parking lot. A moment later, Bruce was unaware, as he walked through the parked cars, that he was being watched from the windows above. He did not know that someone was watching him get into his car, or that his westerly direction was being monitored. He felt self-righteous and as if everything were right in his world.

As Francesca stepped away from the window, and headed back to her dictation room, a code blue was called overhead, "Code blue ICU 32. Code blue ICU 32." Francesca sprinted down the hall toward Rose's room, and saw several staff was already there. As Ruth performed CPR on Rose, the monitor screeched alarms and recording V-fib: Rose's heart was not beating but instead was quivering, as Francesca and the ICU team, pumped and shocked her heart for thirty-eight minutes until it stopped, and they pronounced Rose 'dead.' Barry looked at his gold watch with a big, red secondhand and announced. "Called at 0532."

Francesca said, "I want an autopsy," as she turned to look out the window, in the direction she had just been glaring. She added as an after-thought, "Be sure to send extra intravenous line from her arm. I want to know what was injected into it." She let the ICU team take over, as she returned to that same window, she stood in thirty-eight minutes earlier. She knew the ICU team was busy, and not watching her, so with her back to them, she looked westerly as her fangs protruded.

Her shift was nearly over, and the sun would rise in a couple hours, so Francesca finished her electronic charting, headed to her car, and drove toward Moore funeral home. She had the next three days off and was happy to get away from the human drama of the hospital. After a brief visit at the funeral home with Patrick, she drove toward her quiet street in Virginia Highland and saw the neighbors' sprinklers come on, heard dogs barking, and caught a glimpse of the moon shining through the trees of its last few moments before sunrise. Its early morning hour was the quietest in the area. She could think and plan clearly.

As she turned onto her street, she saw and smelled the familiar houses of her neighbors. Virginia Highlands was an old and refined community in Atlanta. It was established in the twentieth century, but Francesca's house was built in the mid-1800s. Most of the homes had been remodeled, with fine, manicured lawns and gardens. The interiors of the homes were fine woods, grand archways, newly installed central heat, and air conditioning, and all the fineries allowed in historic homes. The young, urban population took advantage of the artistic culture in Atlanta, and of their incomes to preserve and improve a small piece of southern history.

When Francesca awakened the next evening, she already knew what her night would entail. Since it was still dusk, she stayed in her underground quarters and prepared. She was capable of being outside during dusk and early-morning hours, as long as she remained fully covered, but had chosen to wait and get her supplies ready. She has always been thankful to the vampire who invented sunscreen in 1946, as it has also helped her to tolerate the sun. She pulled her black backpack out of its drawer, packed a large pair of prosthetic jaws, a plastic bag, and headed upstairs.

She did not know where Bruce lived, and chose not to Google his address. She relied on her keen sense-of-smell and planned to head out on foot. The sky was overcast with thick clouds, which made the night darker and made her job easier. With her fast movements and her black attire, no one would notice her. It was quickly sundown and she was ready.

She had already put on a sleek, black running suit and shoes, and tied her long red hair into a simple ponytail. She then strolled into the yard, faced Southwest, and stood motionless. She waited as she sorted through the scents of the city as they washed over her. Occasionally, she would tilt her head only slightly to the right, as she sampled the air. There were thousands of aromas from so many places as the breeze shifted, that it took all her concentration to sort them out. She had gotten his scent at the hospital, and she would not forget it. She knew how to wait for it, and so she stood for ten minutes, then twenty minutes. Finally, her brow stiffened. "There you are," she purred, as a half- smile parted her lips, revealing a full set of snow white, needle-sharp fangs. "Now I've got you."

She jogged through her neighborhood toward the scent. As she passed her few neighbors out after dark, she waved back and said *hello*. To any of them, she seemed like just another fit runner, but as she left Virginia Highlands behind, and entered more deserted areas, she ran faster and faster. She would have run faster still, but she had to be careful not to lose his scent. She ran farther west and outside the 285-perimeter than she might have, to avoid jet exhaust from the airport, which was particularly distracting to her keen sense of smell. The jet fuel was harsh and usually overwhelmed any other smells in the area. At one point, she almost lost the scent when she crossed the path of a tractor trailer carrying chickens. "Aaaaaah" She giggled to herself, "Francie, almost got careless to poultry." And then she smiled her half-smile, struck by the irony of one of her kind being thwarted by a truck full of egg-laying birds, but by then she was closer, focused back on her target scent, and on she ran.

Soon after arriving at Bruce's house, she knelt under an oak tree in his yard, and waited. She had to be sure he was alone. She turned her ear toward the window and listened. She could hear the television blaring: He was watching a football game, and she heard the "pssstttt" of a bottle of beer opening. She waited for a second bottle to open; but heard only a single bottle: *no company?* When she heard his footsteps as he walked into the kitchen, she heard no comments to or from another: *no company indeed*, she decided. She tried to identify any other scent, but although she was certain that Bruce had a raccoon living in his attic, there was no sign of anyone else at home. When she was sure, she moved silently up the tree.

Bruce was following his normal, nightly routine: slouched in his recliner, drinking several beers, and watching TV. This time it was a football game, Atlanta vs New Orleans. Bruce had played football in high school, linebacker, and had been rather good, but was almost expelled from school for fighting over a girl. He was recruited by several universities, and it looked for a while like his dream might come true: as he had accepted a scholarship at the University of Georgia. But during his freshman year's division championship game, he got into a fight with an opposing team member, broken his jaw, and he was not allowed back into the school. No other university was willing to take a chance on him, so he lost any opportunity of a continued scholarship. What he did get was extremely angry and even more violent, emotions that he could never quite overcome.

Tonight, he was especially interested in winning because he had money on the Falcons. They were ahead at halftime, and Bruce was feeling rather good (which might also have been due to him being on his fourth beer). In the middle of chugging down his beer, a special news report interrupted his game to announce a brutal rape victim found not far from his house, and before he could catch the details, he thought he heard a mild 'thump' on the roof.

Is that raccoon back again? Bruce thought, but it seemed a little too heavy for that; maybe it was a tree branch, "Either way, I may need to put out another trap tomorrow." His thoughts were interrupted by the sound of shattering glass coming from the back of the house. "Goddamn it! Now what," Bruce swore, as he got out of the recliner, beer in hand, and went to the bedroom. He came out with his baseball bat and headed toward the back door. He unlatched the back door, flipped the light switch but when the light did not come on, he clicked the wall switch up and down several times, and peeked out through the screen. Nothing. He opened the screen door to check the failing light and realized that the bulb had been smashed. He stepped out onto the landing and let the screen door slam behind him, leaned against the railing, and pointed the bat toward the yard. "Who's out there?" he yelled.

A female voice hissed, seeming to come from everywhere at once, "Is that the bat you used on Rose?"

"What?" Bruce shot back, spinning in a circle looking for the source, "Who is that?"

"How is Rose doing now?" the voice asked.

Bruce raised the bat over his head like he was ready to hit a home run. "Come out where I can see you. Rose is fine. I'll see her in the morning!"

"Yeah, that's what you think. You'll be seeing her sooner than you think," she continued to hiss. Francesca reached down from the roof and grabbed the bat out of Bruce's hand. She held the edge of the roof with two fingers and swung down. Her knees caught Bruce square in his face, and he crashed onto the wooden deck and landed hard on his back, his head hitting the floor. His beer bottle shattered on the side of the house. Francesca pounced onto the landing and onto Bruce's chest. Her left knee pinned his right arm, and her right hand pinned his left arm, as he tried to push her off, but he felt like he was bolted to the floor. With one hand Francesca pushed his face onto the floor and exposed his neck.

"Rose is dead, you filthy human, and you're going to join her," Francesca hissed. She opened her mouth wide and sank her sharp fangs into his throat, piercing his jugular vein, as he tried to reply. She knew precisely where his carotid artery was. She knew how to locate it with one movement. She knew not only as a vampire but also as a medical doctor with fine-tuned anatomy skills. As the life flowed out of Bruce, the television blared in the living room, showing a replay of the Saints' go-ahead touchdown over the Falcons in the third quarter. "Yep, I was right. O positive." Francesca swallowed the last of her dinner, before smelling the night air for potential humans involved in the news bulletin she had just heard.

She thought back to the news bulletin. She was sure the announcer had said the latest victim was Ruth Pointer. *Does she know this latest rape victim? Is that her nurse Ruth?*

Chapter 3

Atlanta's newest medical examiner, Dr. Ben Waters, had requested a transfer from Chicago and was granted the move. He had autopsied several bodies in his six months in Atlanta but spent extra time with patients such as the one he just completed. This was the sixth pit-bull attack he had seen in the area since he arrived.

Ben was a tall and muscular man with a touch of grey hair in his full head of brown, wavy locks. At six feet five inches, he demanded attention when he entered a room. His brow seemed to always have a look of determination, which kept his co-workers curious and distant. They did not know if he was a hard, serious doctor, or if he had an agenda. He did not reveal many personal details to them. He did not tell them he lived alone in a small apartment, or that he walked three miles to work every morning.

He sat at his desk on this hot, summer day, and began his dictation into a small recorder. He preferred documenting this way, because he didn't want to take the time to type and hated the new voice-dictation the government had purchased in which he speaks into the computer's microphone and it types his words as he speaks. He tried it a few times and grew tired of the numerous mistakes the transcription made, forcing him to re-speak into the microphone until it captured the correct words. He paid a company in India to receive his tape, electronically, and type it by hand, then email it back to him the next morning completed. He would then have the office workers scan it into his medical charts.

This particular warm morning, he began his dictation, "Patient's name: Bruce Walker, age: thirty-five, weight: 152 pounds, height: five feet, nine inches, race: Caucasian. This gentleman was sent to the Atlanta Medical Examiner with a large, open wound to his right, anterior neck. The wound measures eight inches by six inches and is five inches in depth. The dermis, epidermis, hypodermis, sternocleidomastoid muscle, scalene muscle, external and internal jugular veins, thyroid veins, and vagus nerve have been severed, removed, and absent from the patient and apparently also absent from the scene of the attack. The entire exterior wound has serrations in the dermis consistent with a pit-bulldog bite. There are no other signs of trauma. The entire circulatory system is almost completely void of blood." He paused, looked up at the dusty light on the ceiling. He then rewound the tape and deleted his last sentence regarding any amount of blood.

As Ben completed his report, he knew it contained many unanswered questions; as there was almost no blood at the scene; the ground was almost completely clean; there was no dog hair found, and there was little sign of struggle. If the media knew these bodies had little blood remaining in their bodies, they would have a heyday with the story. As he began to send his report to India to be typed, he heard the announcement of a 'special report' from a small television across the hall. The reporter interrupted the morning news, and was interviewing a local police officer, Detective Franks, who had been at the scene of the attack.

With several microphones on the podium in front of detective Franks, he began to speak, "We have another apparent pit-bull attack in the Atlanta area. It appears this pit-bull might be the same dog as the previous attacks in recent months. We still have no reports of sightings of the dog. Please use caution when outdoors and do not dismiss any pit bulldogs as the attacker. It is a myth that well-raised, nice pit bulls do not attack. This breed was genetically developed to attack and almost all pit-bull attacks are from well-raised, well-mannered, sweet, and loving pets which; for reasons unknown, snap and attack their owner, friends, or neighbors."

When the news story changed to a recent alleged, serial rapist and the search for him, Ben chuckled under his breath, returned to his office, and sent his report. He knew the comments about most attacks being from well-raised pit-bull terriers was accurate, and he also knew that's the only information detective Franks got correct in his media statement. "Oh, the rednecks here will have a hillbilly fit over that statement," he muttered. His brow took on an even more intense look of determination. He turned to look out the window and through the dogwood trees into the distance. With a slight half-smile on one side of his lips, he knew he was getting closer.

*****

As Francesca turned off her seventy-inch plasma screen, she looked worried. Her cheeks were always rosier after such a large attack, but her glow did not cover her apparent fear of someone discovering her, with all this news coverage. She paced silently around her beautiful home. "No one could possibly find me. They're chasing a dog, not a vampire," she mumbled to herself. She shrugged her shoulders and headed to her elaborate basement. She knew she would have to add some new and varied prosthetic pit-bull jaws to her collection to make the attacks appear like different dogs.

The state-of-the-art elevator took her fifty feet below the house, which from the outside looked well-kept, but did not reveal its true extravagance. She had collected some of the world's finest art and furnishings over the past two hundred years, which would be exceptional in a museum. Francesca's affinity for fine and beautiful furnishing was almost equal to her savage deep-seated urges. The original wood baseboards and crown molding were all restored and shimmered in the soft lighting. The fine wood floors were made from local carpenters in 1899, and the only portions of her perfectly maintained home that were not original were the granite counters from local merchants

Most of the fine upholstery was original on the crafted wood chairs. All her furnishings were made of oak and were hand carved. French, woven tapestries hung in each room. All the fine, antique furniture led to the secret and modern elevator that could have passed for a NASA rocket ship, nestled secretly in the middle of her home, and cutting deeply through the granite underneath.

She had fed on cruel and abusive men for two centuries and had never been suspected. She managed to secretly rid the world, to a degree, of men whom she believed deserved to die, and fed on them happily. To feel their hot blood surging through her gave her a feeling of heroism and justification. She would not stop. Her fangs began to emerge just thinking about it, and an evil smile crept across her flawless face, but her eyes still shined with kindness. She kept her anger only for her victims. These yearnings were never satiated. She knew her plight to help her patients and avenge their abusers was a risk, but she was not afraid. Her distaste for men grew with each vengeful attack.

She gathered her wax supplies and began to create several more prosthetic jaw sizes. This process would take several days to complete, as once the wax molds were shaped, and allowed to dry, she would add melted metals to complete a strong pseudo-jaw that mimicked the pit-bulls wide and strong mouth, and that was capable of wedging out and covering up the true infliction in her victims: her own fangs. She would clamp the fake jaws into the fang wound of the already-dead victim and removed any sign of a vampire, leaving only a gaping dog bite. Francesca, with a sense of humor, would throw the removed portion of the neck into the yard of a real pit-bull. These pieces of human flesh have always been devoured by the dog.

Francesca recalled when she did not need such prosthetic jaws to cover her tracks. In 1864, not far from here, the battle of Atlanta raged amid the American Civil War. Slave owners made up a large part of the Confederate Army. She would watch from afar as the slave owners overworked, abused, raped, and took advantage of these people and their freedom in every way imaginable. Occasionally she would wander through the woods after dark and hear the cries of the slaves as the plantation owners would beat and rape them in their meager quarters.

The battle of Atlanta marked the night of fighting, not only for the north and south, but also for the humanity of the slaves, as Francesca took it upon herself to attack these plantation owners in the dark. The battles allowed her to drink from these self-righteous men and throw them into the battlefields. She did not have to cover her tracks then. No one questioned her deep fang marks in the necks of these confederates. She would also often wait outside the slave quarters for the owners to step out into the dark half-dressed after having their way with these women. She lurked in the dark, stealthily went to them and lifted them in the air with one arm, throwing them into the woods and slamming them into the trees. She would lift them up again and let them look into her eyes and allow them to see her fangs protruding down as she held them with one hand and sank her teeth into them.

Although the violence and viciousness of humans had changed a great deal since then, in many ways it had not changed at all. The United States population at that time was 31,000,000. Slaves in the South made up forty percent of the population. Today's population was 331 million; ten times greater than the days of slavery. Today's media assured the community saw the level of crime and violence, and yet they did not point out this giant population growth and the fact that the percentage of crime remained virtually unchanged in humans; it was just more publicized.

She was sure they had announced her coworker and friend Ruth as the latest serial rape victim. She had been ignoring this crime and this criminal because he had not crossed her path. Unfortunately, for him, he just entered her radar.

*****

Ben turned the TV off and returned to his cases for the day. As he tuned into the news of the latest attack behind him and focused on his work, he knew his obsession with these cases could interfere with his work-performance and schedule.   He had quotas to meet, and Atlanta never lacked in dead bodies to be examined. He knew that although the Atlanta area is one of the most beautiful in the country; with its flowers, rolling mountains, cascading greenery, and beautiful buildings, most any other part of the country is a safer place to live, but amidst all Atlanta's beauty and violence, he knew he was getting closer still. Closer to *her*.

Chapter 4

With two hours before dawn and one hour before her shift ended, Francesca headed to the cafeteria to take a break, and appear to be eating a snack. The media and locals had seemed to forget the most recent dog attack. There was no kitchen staff on at this early morning hour, so she bought a whole-wheat breakfast bar from the vending machine and filled a Styrofoam cup half full of coffee. If anyone saw her, they would assume she had drunk some of the old, strong coffee, and was nibbling on her snack.

It was a perfect cover, as moments later, Barry shuffled in, and looking tired and over-worked. Francesca invited Barry to join her. She has always liked Barry and thought he was not only a nice and confident man, but also an excellent registered nurse. His job was not easy in the ICU, as he demonstrated tonight. Barry accepted her invitation and plopped into the seat across from her with his lunchbox from home and released a heavy sigh. He opened it and removed his orange juice and a raw potato.

The rape and death of Ruth had left them puzzled, sad, angry, and exhausted. They sat in silence for several minutes as they tried to process the knowledge of Ruth never working with them again. Francesca was also silently planning her visceral investigation of this elusive rapist. She had been thinking, throughout her night shift, that although she would listen to the police clues broadcast on the news, she would rely on her keen sense of smell, sight, hearing, and then finally taste. She refocused on Barry who seemed to be lost in his own thoughts as well.

Francesca looked puzzled at the potato, and she could not figure out what he would do with it. She had not eaten food in a long time, but she was sure she remembered that humans do not usually eat raw potatoes. When Barry realized that Francesca was staring at his meal, he laughed and chimed in, "You're obviously wondering what in the world I'm doing with a raw potato. It is simple. I always have one in my locker for shifts like tonight. They last a long time, and I can microwave it to perfection in a few minutes, then add whatever toppings I have. It is an ICU trick to survive a rough shift like this. Just like the big, red second-hand on my watch makes it easier to count the heart rate and breaths on our patients, Barry tapped his gold watch. Every little trick helps."

"Genius," Francesca said, with a crooked smile, remembering her raw potato she took to school as a girl. As Barry stepped to the microwave and leaned on the counter to wait three minutes, he turned to look at her. She was throwing her wrappers away and returning to the table. "Barry," she said softly, "thank you once again for all your great help tonight and every night. You deserve a raise. I hope you never take that director position, you're so valuable as a bedside nurse."

Barry sat down again with his steaming meal, pulled some grated cheddar cheese from his lunchbox, and sprinkled it onto his potato. The smell was wonderful, but only to Barry. "My pleasure, Dr. Philips," Barry said with a weary voice, "I love what I do and can't imagine being an administrator. I think they're out of touch with reality in the intensive care." He blew on his hot, steamy potato, jabbed a fork into it, and shoved a large bite into his mouth.

When Barry had had enough of his meal and knew they would need to finish their work in the ICU, they both meandered through the tables and out of the cafeteria and toward the elevator. The elevator-small-talk, took an awkward turn when Barry blurted, "Dr. Philips, you are so beautiful inside and out; your boyfriend is a lucky man." He realized he was speaking out of place and looked down at his shoes. He could not bear to look Francesca in the eyes to see if she were annoyed at his outburst. He was shocked at his own words, and Francesca knew this was a ploy to discuss her boyfriend or lack-of boyfriend status.

"Thank you, Barry, but there's no boyfriend" was Francesca's only reply. His words stirred an old, familiar emotion she had not felt in many decades. She also felt embarrassed for Barry. She knew he had taken a chance with such a bold statement. When the elevator doors opened to the ICU, and they silently stepped out, turning in opposite directions toward their desks, Francesca stopped and turned back, "Barry, would you mind walking me to my car when we finish here? I get nervous when I'm alone in the parking lot."

Barry had been in the ICU for only three years. He had trained as an Air Force nurse, where he had served in Afghanistan and Iraq. He had seen plenty of serious injuries, and yes, blood and death, in his time with the Air Force. He enjoyed working in the ICU because it gave him the same sense of urgency he had as a medical officer.

A grin grew across Barry's face. "Sure, I'd be happy to! Meet you here in half-hour?" Francesca nodded timidly, smiled shyly, and spun back around to head to her dictation room. She had a few remaining charts to sign, one patient to round on, and emails to read. She could easily do this in thirty minutes and meet Barry at the elevator; so why did she regret asking him to escort her to her car? She was in no danger in the dark parking lot. There was no one more dangerous than her. If anything, she would be protecting Barry in the dark. Why should she trust Barry any more than any of the other men who had betrayed and lied to her over the centuries?

Exactly a half-hour later both were at the assigned elevator, and eager to get home. Both acted slightly nervous but knew each other well enough and long enough to cover their new emotions. They were soon in the parking deck at Francesca's Mazda. Again, Barry was looking at his shoes, and his words stumbled. Francesca knew of his nervousness and decided to help the poor guy out. She gave him a friendly hug, kissed him slightly on the cheek, and said, "Thank you, Barry. You have made me feel safe. Drive safely."

Barry returned the smile, "My pleasure." He turned and headed toward his car a few feet away. He whistled, and grinned as he turned the key, backed out, and headed home. He had always felt nervous while talking to Dr. Philips for any reason besides work, but she was easy to talk to, and truly a delight to be with. He felt he had made some great progress.

Francesca decided not to go directly home. Since it was just before sunrise, she strolled into Moore Funeral Home to see her friend. Knowing her way around in the quiet and somber corridors, she made her way to the back hall where the embalming rooms were tucked away from family members to see. There were no signs or windows on the heavy, thick doors. She expertly entered the correct combination into the thick lock on embalming room number three. As she entered, she gazed around to look for bodies. When there were not any, she went to the cabinet on the back wall that was filled with beakers, basins, needles, tubing, and hazardous-waste bags. She reached under the third cupboard door and entered a combination into a hidden lock.

She stood back and waited while the entire cabinet slid backward on a track into a dark hallway. She entered just before the unit slid back into place without a sound. She stood in the darkness, smelling for her friend Patrick. He had always smelled of forest musk and embalming fluid. She knew he was probably already in his chamber for the day. She called his name as she turned a corner and descended a long, dark staircase, which was only lit by a small candle. She often wondered why Patrick lit and maintained these candles, as the only people who used this staircase did not need light. She always assumed it was his way of saying she was welcome, as she had visited him here for eighty years. He made it appear as if he had handed the business down to his grandson, but it was him the whole time. He knew the local humans would wonder how he could live so long and not age. He simply dressed differently: younger, and no one suspected.

Whenever Francesca felt the burden of living amongst humans and feeling a little low on blood, she would visit her dear, old friend. He was the one man she felt had not ever betrayed her and always had fatherly advice for her, since he was 850 years older than her. He had a plentiful supply of blood in storage; as he would drain the blood from his freshly killed patrons and store it, before he would prepare them for their casket, and display them for their funeral. If they had been dead more than one day before arriving at his funeral home, the blood would be too rancid to save for food. Since he picked up most of the fresh deaths at Atlanta Southern Hospital, he always had a fresh supply, as it was no coincidence that most of Francesca's patients were sent to him.

Patrick was sitting in a large and elaborate room with a wine glass full of warmed blood. When he heard Francesca entering the room, he pulled another glass from the shelf, filled it with blood from the warmer, and handed it to her as she gracefully walked into the room. He knew her favorite wine glass, her favorite blood type to drink, and what time to expect her; for they had met in his underground chambers for many decades.

Patrick thought of Francesca as the daughter he never had. He knew of her struggles throughout her entire vampire life, and he knew a little about her life as a human. She had confided in him over the years about Philip, about how she ran away from her family when she became a vampire, about how she yearned for a male companion, but always found them to be liars, cheaters, insecure, and deceitful. He knew not to try to change her mind about human men, because he knew she was mostly correct. Patrick knew of her opinion of human men was connected to her secret, vigilante crusades. "Good evening," in a deep and raspy voice was how he always greeted her.

He gave up drinking fresh blood directly from humans eighty years ago when he opened his funeral service business. He was content to drink from the deceased, and rarely missed the hot, fresh blood, or the rush of sinking his fangs into live flesh. He knew Francesca craved and desired the thrill and pursuit of drinking from live humans, and she felt great satisfaction in attacking villains, particularly male villains.

They sipped the drinks, spoke of their night's work, and laughed. Patrick was the only man Francesca trusted. He had always been there for her. He had mastered the illusion of appearing human as a vampire. He helped her with this illusion to get through medical school, to fit in human society, and he gave her the courage to work in the intensive care with humans.

She was the only other vampire he had contact with. He too, worked in an all-human environment, although many of them were dead. He did not worry about the deceased's family noticing his pale complexion, or his darkened eyes, because they were too busy mourning the loss of their loved one.

"Francesca, you must forget about your human friend, Ruth. You must not pursue this human rapist. Leave human business to humans. You risk revealing your identity enough already," Patrick became serious.

"I will try, but he has now killed my friend and colleague," Francesca replied while sipping from her glass. "I will try to take your advice, but if I catch his scent, I will not ignore it. Now, tell me more about the old days and your current funerals."

Francesca laughed and delighted in his stories. She could find humor in his lifestyle and delighted in his recollection of families changing their views of the deceased to "saintly." She thought it funny that the cheating husband, found dead in his mistress's bed; would be mourned so much by the faithful wife, and that the family and friends would only remember the good things he had done, and forget the bad. She figured this forgetfulness and forgiveness was a trait that humans had that she had lost long ago.

After hours of conversation, and three glasses of warm blood, Francesca kissed Patrick on the forehead and headed home. Since it was daytime, she plastered on extra sunscreen, pulled her large hat over her face and ears, pulled on her long gloves, and headed to her car. She incorrectly felt her life was secure and 'in order.'

Chapter 5

Ben had a full day in store for him. A woman's body, a Jane Doe, had been brought in during the night that had been savagely beaten and raped. Ben had seen a similar case a month ago and tried to keep this case objectively separate from the previous victim. Beside the woman's body was a photo of her taken recently at a party. She appeared young, had a big smile, and seemed to be happy amongst her friends. When his eyes panned over to her lying on the table, her face appeared nothing like the photograph. It was swollen, bruised, cut, and covered in blood and dirt. "These always seem to come here during a full moon," he mumbled, half-kiddingly to himself.

As Ben began his external, head to toe assessment, he spoke into his recorder. "Patient appears in her early twenties, Caucasian, and approximately one-hundred-twenty pounds. There is dirt and twigs embedded in her hair and scalp, to be sent to forensics. There is a deep laceration across her forehead, left eyebrow, left eyelid, left cheek, and extends to her left jaw just below her left ear. Her right eye is swollen shut and bruised. Both nostrils are packed with what appears to be soil and gravel. Her mouth is open, five teeth are missing on the upper right, and two loose teeth are visualized in the back of her throat." Ben continued to describe the numerous injuries from this woman's attack. He assumed she had been raped as he collected what appeared to be semen. Ben dictated that this woman had soil and gravel embedded in her fingernails, indicating she had struggled and clawed at the ground to escape. She has twelve large bite marks to her torso and right scapula area. "Geez, how many attack dogs can one city have?" he said out loud to himself.

As Ben continued to examine the body, he could hear the news from the TV blaring from across the hall. It was Detective Franks again with a special news report regarding last night's rape victim. "The body has been identified, but we are awaiting notification of family members before releasing any information.

This attack is remarkably similar to last week's rape and murder, and we are assuming these two cases are related. I encourage all women and men to stay in the safety of their homes." Detective Franks thought of his own daughter.

Ben strained to hear the news report as he continued to examine the body. He collected and sent soil samples from her hair, scalp, fingernails, and various other parts of her body to the forensics lab for analysis. He also sent pubic hair samples, vaginal contents, and various other debris embedded into this poor victim. By the time he had finished the autopsy the special news report had ended. He knew they had identified her body and he would find out by the end of the day what her name is.

*****

Before getting ready to go to sleep, Francesca sat on her front porch looking up at the stars. She heard a familiar female voice from next door call out, "Hi Francesca!" It was Sally her next-door neighbor, who Francesca had known for many years. Sally was a sweet and cheerful barista in Buckhead, and always smelled of light and flowery perfume. Sally stayed in her grandmother's home while she was in a nursing home. She kept the home and good repair, maintained the meticulous lawn, and visited her grandmother every day after work.

"Hey Sally," Francesca replied, "Come on over for a glass of wine." Sally walked across the two front lawns picking a daisy from her garden and handing it to Francesca. Francesca went inside and returned with the flower, a nice glass of wine, and crackers for Sally. The two have spent several evenings on one of their front porches catching up on each other's lives. Francesca learned that Sally just recently enrolled in college to major in business, and she planned to start in the fall. Sally was especially excited to tell Francesca of her new boyfriend, Dave. "Dave is so wonderful; he calls me every morning to make sure I slept well. He brought me lunch today, and I'm meeting his parents next weekend," Sally said with sweet excitement.

After an hour, Francesca asked Sally to say hello to her mom for her in the two parted ways to retire for the night. Francesca did not usually sleep at night, but her recent busy schedule had made her tired. She thanked Sally for the pretty flower, gave it one more sniff, and went inside. She put the flower in a small glass of water and sat it on the kitchen windowsill. She still loves simple and beautiful flowers as she did as a young girl.

As Francesca got ready for sleep, she listened to the same special news report. She rolled her eyes when hearing of the latest rape victims and the violence in Atlanta. She was not going to get involved. She did not even want to hear the details and turned the television off. She crawled into bed and planned on dozing off immediately, but her mind was busy with the thoughts of work and her patients.

Her mind swirled and she let out a small sigh when she thought of the family members who could not let their very elderly loved ones die peacefully. She was amazed at the selfishness they must put these elderly people on ventilators and other life-support, just to provide a torturous and delayed death. She knew these family members had good intentions, but also knew these intentions were for their own welfare and not for the good of the patient. Mostly her thoughts were of Ruth tending to these patients and how she is going to keep her promise to Patrick and try not to pursue this killer.

Her dreams drifted back to 1838 and the tragic memory now known as the Trail of Tears. Francesca was there when thousands of Cherokee people were forced to walk nearly 1000 miles from North

Georgia to Oklahoma. Over 4000 of these innocent people died of starvation and disease. Francesca did the trek with them from a distance, walking out of sight along their path in the dark, resting in a secluded place during the day, easily catching up with them the next evening, in an effort to find a way to save these people.

She did manage to lure a few of the men working under President Andrew Jackson into the woods but would not kill them. She would allow them to see her fangs, she would act as if she were going to bite them, but instead would ask them if they felt right and humane carrying out such orders. She would ask them how it would feel if it was their family being marched to a reservation without choice. She asked them if they looked into the eyes of these mothers and children as they were being escorted off their native lands. She wanted these men to go back to their jobs questioning their own intent.

She knew killing these men would not change the situation. It was very frustrating as she marched with these families and watch them be bullied by federal and state militia while being forced to leave their homes of many generations. She watched one quarter of these humans die on the trail from starvation and exhaustion. The soldiers would bury them in unmarked graves all along the trail, and since Francesca felt she could do nothing else, she would go behind and mark the graves with a stone formation and wildflowers. She grew weary and hungry throughout the march.

When she awakened, she remembered one group of Cherokees that remained in North Carolina. She was thankful these people survived and to her knowledge still thrive. She smiled to herself before rising out of bed and thought, I must travel to North Carolina soon and visit this community. She rolled over and hoped to have thoughts of Philip taking over her dreams, but the latest newscast haunted her mind. What was it that felt oddly disturbing about these rape cases?

Chapter 6

Soft breezes blew through the trees and flowers as Francesca and Philip ran through the field while holding hands. The pink flowers bent under their bodies as they fell into a pile and while the two laughed and looked up at the passing clouds. Philip ran his hands through Francesca's red, shimmering hair as the sun shone through it. He leaned down, with his muscles straining and kissed her gently, as a dog barked in the distance. He whispered "I'll never leave you. I love you. I will protect you. Trust me. You will never have to run; you will never have to run. Run, run. He is coming. He's coming."

Francesca sat up in bed, recovering from the dream she had frequently. The words whispered even after she awakened. After staring at the ceiling for several minutes, she finally awakened fully from sleeping many hours and jumped into the shower. It was nearly dusk, and her night shift started soon. As she dried and dressed, the images of her vivid dream began to fade. She had grown accustomed to this fun in the field, the sound of Philips whisper in her ear, the smell of the flowers, the distant barking of a dog. She locked her cabinets containing her handmade, prosthetic pit bull jaws, made her bed, and called Patrick. They had checked in with each other every week for nearly two hundred years. Before the invention of the telephone, they visited in person more often. Even though she was a strong and ruthless vampire, when necessary, Patrick insisted on knowing she was safe, and never coming close to conveying her identity to anyone. He knew this potential exposure would be her ultimate death. He hated that she worked so closely with humans, as one wooden stake through her heart would end her life and change his own life forever.

With the sun fully down, Francesca could relax and drive to work. Her walk from the parking deck, through the lower bowels of the hospital, and up the employee elevator allowed her to avoid running into her patients' family members, who inevitably had many questions, and took a lot of her time. As she entered the ICU, the rushing nurses, alarms blaring, and beeps chiming made her feel at home and she forgot her dream of Philip. She received a report from the day-shift doctor, who informed her there is an admission in the emergency department that would be arriving soon.

As soon as she received this report, the elevators opened, and four emergency department staff members pushed in the patient equipment that connected her to the thread of life she clung on to. Barry was already in the ICU room, setting up the ventilator, arranging the equipment to make room for all the staff members to hand-off this young lady. Her transport ventilator was being run by portable battery, she had six IVs hanging from three poles attached to her bed, and four highly trained staff members keeping her alive long enough to transfer her into her specialty ICU bed.

Apparently, the emergency room staff had identified this unfortunate young lady of having a blood sugar of sixteen upon arrival. This, as Francesca knew, is fatally low. There were no other family members or friends present with the patient as she was adjusted to her permanent equipment in the room and the transport staff and their equipment left to return to the emergency department. There was, however, a deputy sheriff present with her the entire time. Apparently, this young lady, Connie, was a known intravenous drug user. Connie was a diabetic, young female who kept her insulin in the refrigerator. Her boyfriend had been arrested for emptying her intravenous opioid vial and replacing it with insulin. So, when Connie thought she was giving herself a small dose of narcotics for a quick high, she had given herself a large dose of insulin. Since this was an alleged attack on her life by her boyfriend, she would have this deputy guard throughout her admission.

The evening became challenging, as Francesca and Barry had to give Connie many doses of D50, a high-glucose injection, to keep her blood glucose as close to normal as possible. Soon after each injection, her blood glucose would rise only to drop again to fifteen. After her sixth D50 injection, Francesca got a phone call from an outside friend checking on Connie. Due to HIPAA laws, Connie's precarious state, and the alleged attempt on her life, Francesca informed the caller that no such information would be given. After the male caller became very argumentative, and Francesca refused to divulge any information about Connie, the caller threatened Francesca's life over the phone from a pay phone in the jail.

"Give me the information on my girlfriend, or I will come up there and take care of you myself when you walk out of the building," the caller growled. "I will make bail and come and find you,"

Once the deputy heard of this, a second deputy guard appeared within minutes. This time the guard was for Francesca. So now not only was Francesca taking care of a nearly dead patient who had a guard, but she had a deputy sheriff following her every move. She could not wait for the night to be over. She could not wait to find this caller once he made bail.

As morning drew nearer, and Barry injected the eighth vial of D50 into Connie's IVs, she began to stabilize. The dayshift staff began to trickle in, Barry gave his report to his replacement RN, Harry, for the day, and Francesca did the same to the MD intensivist of the day. She peeked in one last time at Connie who was beginning to breathe. The same deputy who had been there all night remained in the chair next to her. She thanked him for his time, turn to look at her own personal deputy bodyguard, who was now standing with Barry, and both insisted they would walk her to her car.

The three walked to Francesca's car, while Francesca tried not to smile at the thought that either one of these men needed to protect her, but she played along. Once inside her car, the deputy left her on her own, but stood nearby watching for any shady characters. Barry insisted on sitting in her passenger seat for a few minutes and she let him feel macho and protective. She welcomed the conversation, pulled some sunscreen out of her glove box, insisting it was lotion for her dry skin, and continued to talk to Barry for the next hour.

Their conversation was briefly interrupted when Barry's phone rang in his scrubs pocket. "He answered without saying hello and instead said, half laughing, "Oh no, what did I forget?"

The response was Harry laughing and asking, "No, no. Nothing at all. I am just wondering if you have the narcotics box key. We can't find it."

"Oh shit. Yes, I do. It is right here in my pocket. I will bring it back up in a few minutes. Sorry," Barry casually replied to Harry. He hung up and said to Francesca with a heavy sigh, "I've done it again." He held her hands together and said, "please go on with your story."

She continued talking after rolling her eyes in fun, and told him of her love long ago, how he had left her for another woman, how she was heartbroken for a long time until she grew to learn to trust only herself. He agreed with her, maybe a little too easily. She shared quite a bit of the story of Philip except the fact that it was over 200 years ago. Barry asked if she had run into him recently, and she chuckled with a quick "no."

He then confided in her that his mother was abusive and left him with his father when he was just thirteen. He stated he was glad she was gone at that time, because not having her was better than having her there when she would hit him, call him stupid, often forget to make dinner in her drunken state, and force him to fend for himself most of the time.

Francesca and Barry seemed to grow much closer than they even were before. They learned each other's birthdays, their favorite music, places they had vacationed, stories of family members, and many small details that create a bond. When Barry yawned for the fifth time, Francesca said they must part ways and each go home and go to bed. As Barry nodded, the look in his eyes changed to a sincere mood. He tilted his head slightly to the side and said, "May I kiss you?"

Francesca surprised herself when her answer was "Yes." Barry gently leaned in and lightly kissed Francesca. His kiss was so soft and kind, that this too caught Francesca off guard. She did not know she had any surprises left in her. As he opened the car door and stepped out, Francesca could only watch him in silence.

She watched him in her mirror as he walked slowly to his car, fumbled to get his keys out of his pocket, start to put them in the door lock, then arch backwards, saying, "ooooh,"as he remembered he has to go back upstairs with the narcotics key.

Once he was out of sight, she touched her fingers to her lips. She thought of the new development of this friendship, but mostly she thought of the pleasant but odd smell when Barry leaned in.

Chapter 7

As the sun rose, and the full moon set, Ben walked down the long corridor toward his office with a large cup of coffee in his hand. He was whistling a tune he just heard on the radio, and now could not get it out of his head. He stepped into his office, sat his coffee on the desk, spun around into his chair, and checked his email. Once he finished answering last night's emails, he looked at today's work schedule. Apparently, he had two rape victims that have made it to his table during the night, and the song in his head suddenly disappeared.

He clicked on the news, and just as he suspected, these two unfortunate ladies were the headline. Oddly, the Atlanta news interviewed neighbors and witnesses to big stories. They seem to enjoy a close-up of locals with poor grammar and missing teeth. After listening to several neighbors with garbled southern drawls, the newscaster came back on. The two latest victims lived about one mile apart. Their names had not been released yet, but Ben had them on his computer and on their toe tags in the morgue down the hall.

He finished listening to the news report, sipped on his coffee, then finished reading the police reports about the two victims. Apparently, the news got it right that the two victims lived near each other. His report listed the victims ages, next of kin, race, height and weight, and a very brief description of the bodies' conditions. One victim was named Bernice and the other's name was Sally. The report stated they had several small areas of dog bites. Ben mumbled to himself, "Geez, how many dog attacks can one city have?" He assumed these were from the same attacker that left bite marks on the victim's in prior cases. He knew not to jump to conclusions before a thorough autopsy. He clicked his computer off, chug down the last cup of coffee, and headed to his exam room.

He decided to just start with victim number one because she had a number one on her body bag. He pulled her info onto the large computer screen on the wall to compare his findings with her statistics. Ben's assistant, Lori, was already in the room and had prepared all the tools for the day. As Ben unzipped the body bag, Lori gasped. Apparently even medical examiner staff could be caught off guard occasionally. The report underplayed the bite marks on this victim. They were large and gaping holes with obvious teeth marks around each hole in her neck, breasts, abdomen, back, and inner thighs. He scurried over to the closed cooler drawer where victim number two lay waiting. He pulled out the long stretcher that her corpse laid on. He unzipped the bag just to see if she had the same bites. She did indeed have similar bites with the same large gaping tooth marks. He pushed her back into her drawer and latched the cool handle, thinking this did not seem anything like the pit bull attacks.

After doing a thorough head to toe examination, opening her chest and re-closing it, he sent many samples to the lab. He had seen enough rape cases to know her vaginal secretions were semen. He determined her cause of death to be exsanguination due to eighteen large and gaping bite wounds. He found no blunt force trauma, he found no stab or bullet wounds, she did not appear to have died of asphyxiation, she was raped and bled out. He began on victim number two whose bite marks measured the same depth and diameter as victim number one. Her samples were sent to the lab, he opened and closed her with the respect she had not received the night before. His thoughts wandered to these ladies' family members and the horrible and violent loss of their loved ones.

Back in his office, he completed the numerous reports required on each autopsy. His cell phone had been lying on his desk all morning and was now flashing a new voicemail. Ben picked up his phone, listened to the message from Sergeant Franks, noticed he had left twelve of them, and hit "call back." After the fourth ring,

Ben assumed he was going to get a voicemail, and was surprised when Sergeant Franks answered.

"Sergeant Franks, this is Ben Waters returning your call. I see you had a busy night." He noticed Sergeant Franks seemed upset and even winded.

With a shaky voice, Sergeant Franks replied, "Dr. Waters, thank you for calling me back. One of your victims is my daughter, Sally, I called to get an update on your autopsies when you have completed them and verify a cause of death. I am assuming it is the same dog that has been attacking people around Atlanta, right? My daughter had a soft spot for animals," he said as he unsuccessfully tried to hold back the tears.

"Oh my God, I am so sorry. Sergeant Franks, I do not think those pit-bull cases are related to last night's victims, including your daughter, at all. These ladies had several bites throughout their bodies, whereas the pit bull attacks had one large bite to their neck as pit bulls do. I'm sorry to say these ladies were also raped, so obviously there is more than a dog involved." Ben did not discuss with Sergeant Franks the fact that the pit-bull victims were nearly depleted of their blood supply and none was present in their bodies or at the scene, or that these two rape victims were a bloody mess both at the scene and all over their bodies. Ben went to great lengths to assure these details never made it out of his office or onto his reports.

After a long day and no breaks, Ben pulled a peanut butter sandwich out of his desk drawer, quickly ate it, and sipped on a glass of wine. Although the evening news was on, and the two attack victims were still in the highlights, a 'person of interest' named Dave had been mentioned and identified as Sally's boyfriend.

Ben stared out the window at the Atlanta nightlights, and whispered to himself "Where are you? I know you are nearby. Where are you? Who are you? I feel you close by. I see you"

Chapter 8

Patrick handed Francesca a large wine glass filled with fresh, warm blood. Classic piano music played on the gramophone in the background, the warm candle sconces pleasantly lit the room, as the two old friends enjoyed their evenings company. The television was on silently in the background, when Francesca suddenly stood and said, "Turn that up!"

As Patrick increased the volume, Francesca walked closer to the television with her eyes glued on the headlines: "Two women attacked last night in Atlanta." Patrick began to moan a discouraging sigh but was shushed by Francesca. She wanted to hear every word. She listened to how they were probably raped. She listened to the victim's mother's cries as the Atlanta news camera zoomed in on her face and saw Sergeant Franks divulge that one of the victims, Sally, was his own daughter. When Sally's picture appeared, she did not tell Patrick this was her next-door neighbor and friend. She memorized the locations. She was oblivious of Patrick's protesting words. She did not listen to him as he told her to "Leave it alone. Let this one go. You can't punish all the bad guys in the world." She heard none of Patrick's discouragement after hearing the words, *Dave, person of interest.*

Patrick convinced Francesca to sit down and enjoy her blood before it cooled, although she was planning her next move. Patrick was the only male Francesca would listen to. He became a father figure to her many decades ago. He called to check on her after an all-night shift, he sent bags of blood home with her in the cooler, he always assured she has plenty of sunscreen, and he continued to worry about her engaging so much with humans. As much as she hated to admit it, she was very thankful for Patrick and his loving care. His family and friends have been long gone way before she ever even became a vampire. Francesca would try to ignore her instinct to find this killer, even though he just murdered her sweet neighbor. She would try to ignore human activity to please Patrick.

As Patrick poured another glass of warm blood for Francesca, they discussed his funeral business, her intensive care work, the state of humans in present day and their obsession with petty issues and laughed into the night. As the hours clicked by, and the two friends exchanged stories of their week, another special report came across the television screen. This time a thirty-year-old woman was brutally attacked, allegedly raped, bitten, and left in a dumpster. Her body was found in the ditch just outside Tyler Perry Studios. Patrick knew before he even turned his head to look at Francesca that all his calm conversation was just thrown out the window.

Francesca's fangs popped out as she stared at the screen. She was looking in the background at the roads, the driveways, the dumpster, the light posts, any sign of a clue she could use. "I will find this man," she snarled as she spun around and faced Patrick. "He will dread the day he bumped into this woman in the dark," she said with her fangs protruding down over her lower lip, her brow tightened, and clinking her empty glass down on the table.

"It's been a long time since I've had a tasty rapist to feast on. I will make him beg for his life. I will make him see the lives he has taken and the family members he has hurt forever. I will make him dwell in his inevitable demise. I will let him see the fangs that will rip through his carotid arteries and slowly, very slowly, suck the life out of him. I will let him feel every drop leave his body as his heart rate slows until it beats no more. He will hurt no one, no women, once I find him." Her voice was slow, deliberate, and low. Her fangs shined in the candlelight. Her eyes glared at Patrick as she described in detail what she would do to this man.

She reminded Patrick of the time she was at Tyler Perry Studios in the 1870s, at that time, it was Fort McPherson. The Civil War had ended a few years earlier, but not all slaves were yet freed. Many slave owners left no means for independence for these people, as they had no education, they had no way to travel, they had no money, and therefore the plantation owners took advantage of the fact that the slaves had no means to start their own lives of freedom. They continued to keep them as slaves but called them 'workers' instead.

The abuse continued, the beatings continued, the raping continued, and so did Francesca's attacks on these Confederates. Once she had drank the blood of the owners, often while they were leaving Fort McPherson, she would return to their plantation and assist the slaves to the underground railroad even though the war had ended. The underground railroad had continued for these situations, and Francesca led them to the nearest available houses, gave them money and food, provided them with clothing and blankets and shoes.

Francesca found it ironic and rewarding of this history of Fort McPherson, as well as the fact that it housed German Navy prisoners during World War I, and its current situation as a film studio owned by Tyler Perry, who did so many wonderful things for many people of all colors. She thought it as the most perfect transition for such a location and wished those confederates would have known the turn of events their fort would endure.

As the news report of the two rape victims continued, and as protective as Patrick felt of Francesca, he knew no words would stop her. He knew that look. He knew that determination. He knew that fierce vampire that he helped raise from a young vampire-age would find this man and do exactly what she described. He secretly admired this about Francesca but feared her own demise in her bravery. As much as he longed to tell her to stay safe, he sat his now-empty glass of warm blood on the table, reached out and held her hands, and whispered, "Go get him."

Chapter 9

Several days went by, with no more mention of an attacker or rapist. Francesca went to work nightly at her usual time, Barry continued to walk her to her car at the end of their shift, now with a nightly kiss, but tonight was Francesca's night off, and she had agreed to go to a movie with Barry. She was determined to get the rapist before his next attack and went out to her yard, walked over to Sally's yard, stood by the bedroom window until she caught Dave's scent through the glass, and then walked throughout downtown Atlanta smelling the air for a hint of his scent before Barry arrived to pick her up. She lingered in the back yard of Dave's condominium, smelling his scent, watching him through the window, wondering if he was Sally's killer. She memorized his face.

She already missed Sally, and when returning home with no new clues, the police tape that was still wrapped around Sally's porch struck her more so than seeing it from her driveway.

To allow herself time to hunt on this walk, she turned down Barry's offer for dinner before the movie, saying she was on a strict diet of low carbs and did not want to disrupt her routine. Besides, it was always difficult to eat human food. They sat in the back of the theater, and like teenagers on a date, their handholding turned into deep, hot, and passionate kisses. Francesca had not felt this heat from within her in a long time. She surprised herself at how easily she welcomed his warm hand inside her shirt. He caressed her breasts as his deep and hot kisses sent waves of longing through her body.

She found herself undoing his belt and reaching down to caress him as he could barely be contained by his blue jeans. She felt like a young girl in the back of that dark movie theater. They kissed and caressed and learned each other's bodies until the movie credits shined across the screen. As Francesca straightened her clothes, she also looked around to assure that no one had been watching them, but neither one really cared. As they tried to act casual, they walked back to his car, when Barry said, "I should drive you home."

"Yes, I should probably get home, it is getting late," Francesca said still slightly out of breath. She could hear and feel his heart beating, she could smell his blood cursing through his veins, and she swore to herself many decades ago that 'a mistake made more than once is a decision.' She thought to end this with a human man before it got too serious, and that thought flashed through her mind for only a brief second. Human men had never given her anything but pain and betrayal. They looked at each other for one moment, and then she was on his lap and one swift movement. He lowered the seat and moved it back, as she removed his pants to his knees. Barry did not even see that she had already removed hers. She straddled and hovered above him as she kissed him deeply. He moaned in delight. She could feel his sweating body throbbing against her but would not allow him to enter. Not just yet. She wanted to hear him ask for it. She wanted him to beg to be inside her. As the windows fogged over, she got her wish.

She lowered her steamy hot juices onto him. He filled her with a firm and hard release that shuddered through her spine. As he thrust harder and deeper inside her, she forgot all about any concerns that were stressing her throughout her day and night. She only knew about him right here, right now. It was dark enough to hide her fangs which had come out like an orgasm in release. She rode up and down as Barry thrust deeper and harder. They could not get enough of each other. They did not care if anyone heard as they moaned and cried out in delight. The steam on the windows was now so thick it began to drip, just as the juices between them dripped from them and around them.

She had not felt this satisfied since one of her endeavors assisting slaves to the underground railroad. After delivering three slaves to a congressional church in Ohio with food, clothing, and money, she had begun her trek back to Atlanta to rescue more slaves. While walking through the darkness in the mountains of Tennessee, she noticed a strong odor. It was not an unpleasant odor, but when she had never encountered before. It was not long before she came upon a tall gentleman walking on the trail alone.

They talked for several hours, and she had no difficulty hiding her identity in the dark, and he seemed to enjoy the dark as well. The sex lasted all evening. She had not felt such a strong and seductive man until that night. Barry reminded her of that man. His deep moans were the same as well as his deep thrusts. Both men had shaken her to the core like no one else could do. She did not bite the man that night for two reasons; she did not want to give her identity away or kill this man, and although she was very hungry from her long journey with the underground railroad, she was not aware that he had done anything wrong, and rarely did she bite or drink from good people.

She had not thought of this man in many decades and wondered why Barry reminded her of him. She decided at this moment that spending time with Barry would not hurt anyone. She genuinely liked him, and the sex was amazing. She knew not to trust any man, and she knew she would never fall completely in love with anyone, as she lost that desire a long time ago, but her insatiable sexual desire has never dwindled.

Chapter 10

Francesca seemed to forget all about the attacker, as each night she and Barry enjoyed each other's company followed by deep and passionate love. She surprised herself at how easily she let a man into her life, but she looked forward every day to their animalistic sex that evening. They worked together, slept together, played together, and eventually Francesca almost forgot about any revenge on the attacker. A month had gone by and she had spent nearly every night of it with Barry. She even grew accustomed to his occasional odd odor and he assured her he would get a new cologne.

One evening, on her night off, the phone rang, and she happily answered it in an almost singing voice, "Hello?".

"Good evening. My name is Dr. Ben Waters and I am calling for Dr. Francesca Philips."

"I'm Dr. Phillips, how can I help you Dr. Waters?" Before she could get his full name out, the line went dead, and a dial tone was all that remained. She turned the phone over in her hand and looked at it as if it might tell her why this person called or why they hung up. She simply shrugged her shoulders, laid the phone down, and continued to her whistling while drinking a glass of warm blood. She was spending the evening alone as Barry was out of town visiting family for the weekend. As much she enjoyed spending time with him, she also enjoyed being by herself and was overdue to visit Patrick.

The sun had already set, so Francesca took her glass and sat out on her front porch. She enjoyed watching her Virginia Highland neighbors walk up and down the dark streets under the streetlights. She remembered the days of walking with her parents and sisters to church and she smiled with a little sadness in her eyes. The chatter and the laughter from the houses across the street reminded her of sitting on her porch with Philip and laughing. She could hear the silverware clink through her neighbors open windows just as they did two centuries ago while her mother washed dishes, and Philip brought her flowers. She turned her head half-expecting to see Sally walking toward her.

The hours went by as Francesca reminisced about her life long ago and her much-different life now. She saw the full moon creep up above the trees as she wondered how she allowed herself to be involved with a human man and how happy she was with this new development. She could hear Patrick's words in her mind telling her '*you know better than to get personally involved with a human. You know nothing good will come of it. It's difficult for me to keep you safe when you're out mingling with lowly humans and sometimes even in the daylight.*' His voice echoed through her thoughts. She knew he was right but not this time. She knew that those closest to you are the ones who betray you, but not this time. She held her glass up to the moon as if to toast with herself.

As her thoughts of Philip continued, a neighbor dog startled her back to reality with his barking. She jumped in her chair and even spilled a little blood out of the side of her glass. She shook her head, sighed, and went back in the house and turned on her music. The phone rang again, and she knew it was going to be this strange Dr. Waters again. Her voice was not quite as cheerful as she said "Hello?"

She was surprised when she learned it was the charge nurse, Harry, on duty tonight in the ICU. He talked about how the day and evening has gone on Francesca's day off, and how they all missed her when she was not there. He then informed Francesca that the gentleman, who was charged with exchanging insulin into his junkie-girlfriend's opioid vial, was released from jail and the attempted-murder charges were dropped. The girl who had nearly died because she thought she was injecting heroin into her veins, but it was a lethally high dose of insulin, had come to the ICU with a glucose level of sixteen, and had been in a coma, woke up and dropped the charges on this guy. "I wanted you to know the man who threatened you is out of jail," nurse Harry finished.

Harry continued to inform Francesca that her patient, Connie, had been weaned from life support earlier that morning, was discharged by lunch, and after dropping the charges on her boyfriend, had moved back in with him.

"Well, he won't live long," Francesca mumbled.

"What?" Harry questioned.

"I said, he won't be wrong," she quickly lied, and hung up.

Francesca walked to the cupboard that contained all her pit bull prosthetic jaws, and as she pulled the drawer out her fangs also came out. She removed the cloth folded beside the jaws, polished them as if they were silver dinnerware, as her green eyes glared over in red.

She sat waiting outside Connie's home and waited for a glimpse of the man who had nearly killed this young lady. She saw Connie through the window seemingly arguing with someone but could not see him. She could hear a male's voice yelling at her and waited to make her move. The two inside argued for what seemed to be two hours but finally the man came out and got in his car. He backed out of the driveway and headed to the local gas station to restock his cigarettes.

He soon walked around the corner from the gas station with a ring of smoke circling his head, and in a deep sigh of relief as he exhaled the caustic smoke from his lungs. He had not had a cigarette in days, he had not had a hit in days, he had not had sex with Connie or his other girlfriends in days, and these people all owed him for his loss. He walked around to the driver side of his door and opened it only to see two sets of red eyes and two sets of white fangs coming at him before he could even get in.

Chapter 11

Ben scratched his head as he looked down at the newest pit-bull victim. He had one large gaping bite taken outside of his neck, he had been exsanguinated of all his blood, and of course no blood was found at the scene. Surprisingly, this latest victim's neck was also snapped in half, he noted. There was no evidence of any human contact, there were no footprints near his car, there were no fingerprints on or in his car, no witnesses, there were only the similar tooth imprints from the previous attacks in Atlanta. Ben knew there was another dog attack awaiting autopsy for the afternoon. He did not yet know if this one was by a pit bull or by the other dog that bites in several places. He had enjoyed his month of no dog attacks and felt bittersweet that he had one today.

He finished his report on the pit-bull victim with a broken neck and with one large and gaping bite wound to the neck. He omitted the lack of blood in the body and went straight to the next case.

He was indeed correct, in the next case, that this most recent and unfortunate woman had been raped and bitten with large gaping dog teeth over most of her body; in fact, some parts of her torso were even missing. Her left femur was broken, her vaginal tissue was torn, several ribs were broken and two were protruding out of her chest. Does this violent attacker rape her first and then let the dog eat her? Her hair was so covered in blood, he had to wash a small portion of it to see what true color it was. This second patient was obviously not exsanguinated.

He stood over the mangled and bloodied body and thought about his phone conversation with Francesca yesterday. Should he have hung up? Should he have called at all? She did readily identify herself, and he thought that was a big step. How could she be so careless and foolish to expose her identity so easily? He was glad he did not have a conversation with her. He hoped she would pursue finding him since he left his name with her. When she did not, he turned his frustration into his work and finished the autopsies for the day. He dictated all his reports, released them to the police department, and rode his bicycle home.

He walked into his apartment, threw his Mary Mac's takeout onto the counter, and opened the doors to his deck. The nearly full moon shone in through his wispy sheer curtains. Sounds of downtown Atlanta roared through his apartment as he dug into his takeout with his fork and propped his feet on a stack of books on his coffee table. The books were old and worn but Ben seemed too frustrated to care at the moment. A closer look at the worn and faded titles of the books revealed research into mythical vampires.

These books, meant to sound like fiction, described the history of vampires, the religions of vampires, how vampires were created and how they can die. They described fictional vampires by name and date, places they have lived, and the current state of vampires today. These books were labeled 'fiction.' Ben bought them in the 'fantasy' sections of several bookstores from different areas around the world. They were not meant to be taken seriously, but he had spent the past three evenings at Barnes and Noble reading the vampire stories they had as well.

*****

Francesca signed into her evening shift with a new twenty-two-week pregnant patient. This twenty-three-year-old patient's husband was deployed in a submarine, so she stayed with her parents throughout her pregnancy. Her parents were in their forties and were not concerned when their daughter, Sadie, slept late as they left for work. She was pregnant and needed sleep. When her parents returned that evening, Sadie was in bed taking a nap or had gone to bed early for the evening. They still thought nothing of it. The same thing happened the next morning when they went to work, and she was still asleep. They assumed she was awake during the day while they were at work. By the time they arrived the second evening, and she was in bed, they became nervous and knocked on the door. She was unresponsive and would not revive to their voices or the fact that they lifted her and put her in the chair. They called 911 and she arrived in the ICU with a blood sugar of twenty-three. She had been in a diabetic pregnant coma for two days.

Francesca worked through the evening to revive Sadie and get her blood sugar back to normal limits. Barry was working tonight, and Francesca was happy to be working by his side. Their three days apart felt like three weeks. She deeply missed him. Barry exchanged intravenous lines, reset pumps, emptied her Foley catheter, moved her from side to side, and ran all the equipment as an expert would. By the end of their shift, Sadie was beginning to awaken. Her parents had not left her side throughout the night. They called Sadie's husband, which took many phone calls with a special connection to speak with him on the submarine. He now had permission to depart the submarine and head home to be with his wife. Since he was in the South Pacific, this would not be a speedy process.

Francesca and Barry sat in the cafeteria while Barry baked his raw potato in the microwave and then ate it with just butter. Again, he was happy to be working with Francesca and did not even realize he had not eaten all night until the end of their shift. Francesca informed Barry she had managed to sneak down a sandwich and was not hungry at the moment. Barry informed her of his visit with his family, how he and his mother had petty arguments the entire visit, and that he went fishing with his dad. He seemed happy since visiting with his family. He could not stop from smiling and could not keep his eyes off Francesca.

Barry stated he could not spend one more night without her and needed to come over tonight after they both got some rest through the day. He looked surprised when Francesca said she had to take a rain check until tomorrow night because she promised Patrick, she would visit him, as she has not been spending nearly as much time with him lately. She informed Barry that Patrick stated he had something important to talk to her about, and she could not turn him down tonight. Barry's smile change from large and toothy to disappointed and strained. *Did he seem jealous?*

Chapter 12

Francesca was going to go to Patrick's around eight PM but decided to go earlier and attend the latest rape victim's funeral service. She thought maybe she would get a clue or a glimpse of this guy. He was a serial rapist, and the police department was obviously too inept to find him. She thought the serial rapist had moved on, but obviously he had not, and needs her to pay him a late-night visit.

The funeral parlor was full of crying family and friends, and the casket containing a young and beautiful woman. The young lady's mother was sobbing into her husband's arms. He had a look of helpless anger and knew of nothing he could do but hold her. Siblings and cousins delivered the eulogy, her college professor spoke of her wonderful attitude, her 4.0 GPA, her promising career as a teacher. Each word hit the family and friends with reality and horror. This young lady was taken by a cold-blooded killer.

Francesca scanned the room for someone, anyone, who looked out of place. Someone who was not crying. Someone who did not belong. She suspected she might see Dave, Sally's so-called boyfriend. When she could not find such a person, she began to give up when she saw Barry sitting in the far corner. She did not know Barry knew this lady. He had not mentioned it this morning. They made eye contact, and Barry gave her a loving smile from across the room. Francesca could not wait for the eulogies to be over so she could approach him. Once the sobbing mother and father walked up one last time and kissed their daughter on the forehead, the family and friends headed to their cars to make their procession to the cemetery. Francesca used this opportunity to bump into Barry.

"Barry what are you doing here?" Francesca asked with sincerity.

"Oh, hey Francesca. I thought I might see you here. I knew the family when I was young. We were neighbors."

Just then Francesca saw a tall gentleman with a long black jacket duck out the back door. He was muscular and wore a black hat. She did not see his face very clearly, but she was determined she would. She excused herself rather abruptly from Barry and ran out the back door as well. The man was gone, but she tried to catch his scent before it blew away in the wind. She turned to get to her car to chase him, when she noticed Barry standing alone in the doorway. She sniffed the air, then went back to Barry to console him and to comfort him knowing she would catch up to whomever that man was later. Barry seemed uneasy, and she wanted to be with him. He asked her to join him at the cemetery, but Francesca graciously declined stating she still needed to talk to Patrick. She walked him to his car, kissed his cheek, and waited patiently while Patrick wrapped up the process of the day, and finished his book-keeping. He did not go to the cemeteries during the day.

Later that evening, when the funeral services had been cleared and Patrick was free to talk, he met Francesca down deep in his basement. He had a fresh supply of new blood and offered her a glass of type AB-negative, a rare treat and her favorite. She accepted and gave him a warm smile she saved only for him. He seemed much more serious tonight than usual.

"Francesca let me get right to it, he said in his deep and raspy voice. I have been watching the news about these rape victims. That young girl's body upstairs was the latest one. I see something that I have not seen in hundreds of years. I see a pattern that nobody knows but me. I do not think these cops are dealing with a regular serial rapist, and I worry these dog attacks are too similar to yours and might lead the police to you. I want to tell you a story."

Francesca sat up in her chair, both palms wrapped around her wine glass filled with warm blood. Patrick seemed focused about this topic. She had not seen him this serious in a long time. She listened intently.

"Long ago, before you were born, and when I lived in Europe, there weren't just vampires," he began.

Francesca waited for him to go on, but he paused. He could not figure out how to form the words for talking about it might seem to make it become true. "What are you talking about Patrick?"

"There were others." Again, Patrick could barely get the words to come through his lips.

"Geez Patrick, tell me what's on your mind. Tell me what is wrong. Who's raping these women?"

"I haven't seen them in a long time, and I thought they were all gone, but………… werewolves. I think werewolves are doing it."

Francesca let out a laugh but stopped when she saw that Patrick was serious. Now *she* was speechless. She waited for Patrick to continue but he did not. He simply looked her in the eye and let her process this news.

Patrick finally went on, "These werewolves are vicious killers. They chase their victims during a full moon, hunt them down, attack them and rape them, while biting them all over their bodies. They are not selective. They attack young women usually during the two or three days of full moon, but sometimes on other evenings as well. Some of them can grow nearly as strong as a vampire. Of course, they are not immortal, but can be exceedingly difficult to kill. My maker was killed by a werewolf hundreds of years ago because he underestimated their large size and brute strength!"

"I never knew how your maker died! I had no idea. Do you think a werewolf killed Sally?" Francesca asked questions throughout the evening, but still did not comprehend the magnitude of Patrick's prediction. She tried to imagine Dave as a werewolf.

Chapter 13

The next morning Francesca watched the news and fixated on Patrick's theory. Surely, he was wrong. She had never heard of the existence of werewolves. He believed an old myth and tried to get her to back away from pursuing the rapist. She thought how she had argued with him the night before as he tried to convince her that he was correct. She felt bad now that she even laughed at him. She recalled Patrick almost begging her to back away from these rape cases. He informed her these werewolves are much stronger than anyone could imagine. There are even capable of killing a vampire, and they hide in broad daylight.

As Francesca recalled her conversation with Patrick the evening before, checked on the remaining three units of AB-negative blood in the refrigerator that Patrick sent home with her, a special news bulletin flashed across the screen. Another rape victim was found last night but survived the attack. She was currently in the hospital and refused to speak to police about her attacker. She had bite marks all over her body, two broken arms, and a broken jaw. Francesca regretted not following the man in the long black coat rather than consoling Barry during the funeral yesterday. She wondered where to investigate the existence of werewolves. She thought she should start with older books, so she decided to begin her search in Atlanta Vintage Books in Brookhaven.

She recalled the evening on the trail of the underground railroad and how she occasionally heard a wolf howling at the moon light and wondered if those could have been werewolves. She remembered sex that dark evening with that strange man. He was stronger and more robust than most. *Could she be so easily fooled? Could there really be such a thing? Could last night's attacker be a werewolf?* She quickly dismissed all these thoughts and questions as she realized she had some researching to do.

*****

Ben watched the same news bulletin. He felt a little thankful that he would not have this victim on his table today. He wondered if the rapist was getting lazy. This was the first of his victims that had survived. *How did she survive? Why did she survive? Did she fight him off? Did someone discover them and scare him away?* Ben wondered. He knew Sergeant Franks would be questioning her at length today.

His cases consisted of a man in his sixties who died at home of an apparent heart attack and whose wife stated he ate burgers and fries and smoked cigarettes every day. His next case was a gentleman who fell down the stairs at the shopping mall, lived four days on life support, and had an apparent brain bleed because he hit his head and he also took a daily anticoagulant, clopidogrel, an anticoagulant blood thinner that is difficult to reverse quickly. Trauma like this while taking this level of blood-thinners often results in death.

******

Sergeant Franks easily walked past the police guard in into the rape victim's hospital room. The look on his face and the wrinkle in his brow was more stern than normal. Most of her body was bandaged and she was heavily sedated. She did open her eyes to his voice and made little effort to answer his questions.

"Ma'am I'm sorry this is happening to you. I am Sergeant Franks from the Police Department. I am here to help you. Can you tell me about your attacker?" he asked with perhaps a little too much determination.

The unfortunate young lady had already fallen back asleep before he could finish his questions. Despite his attempts to waken her, her mother asked that he stop immediately and let her sleep.

Sergeant Franks and the mother spoke for another hour about where her daughter had been, all her friends and family, where she worked, what she drove, who her boyfriends were, who her enemies were, until every aspect of this young lady's life was discussed. Sergeant Franks asked her if she knew of a man named Dave, and when she denied knowing such a man, he felt as if he had made no progress in getting closer to this attacker. Her daughter worked at Peachtree Branch Library, and the attack apparently happened when she was walking home after dark.

He called the crime lab to see if DNA samples or any other evidence were resulted yet and they had not. He had a guard at her door, a guard at the hospital's main entrance, a guard at each smaller hospital entrance, and more in cars in the parking lots. He wanted to assure if this rapist showed his face anywhere in this vicinity, he would be noticed. He exited slowly out of the room, thanking the victim's mother, and looking into each room as he slowly walked down the hall toward the elevator. He exited the main entrance and stood on the covered circle drive for quite a while until he resigned to the fact that he got little information today and that the facility was well guarded. He missed his daughter and was determined to find justice for her. He would find this man. *Why hadn't he asked more questions about this unknown man, Dave, she had mentioned she was dating?*

Chapter 14

Francesca searched the internet far into the daytime trying to find any information on werewolves. The image of the tall man at the funeral home stayed on her mind. She had just telephoned Patrick to question the guest book that was present at the victim's funeral. She had hoped she could get access to it and read the names for a clue, hoping the rapist had signed it. She was disappointed when Patrick told her he never has possession of the guest book and it goes home with the family immediately after the service. She doubted whether such a person would sign his name on a book anyway.

She found little information on the internet about werewolves and most of it was caricatures and comics. If anyone besides Patrick had told her about the existence of werewolves, she would have already dismissed it. *Could it be true? Could a werewolf be the rapist? Why had she not known about this before? Where could she find some real proof and evidence?* She decided to go to the library.

After buying one book in Atlanta Vintage Books, another book from Read Shop by the Merchant, she visited the library where she found a small section on werewolves. Most were romance stories involving werewolves, and they were almost all checked out. She finally found one mythical book titled "Where Werewolves Were." Despite the cheesy title it appeared to be the closest thing to factual. Chapter one described werewolves in ancient times when they were much more barbaric. Chapter two described how they progressed to appear more human and fool others into trusting them. Chapter three through ten told of stories of attacks, werewolf hunters, and had many drawings of what they were thought to look like. The remaining chapters described how the progression of society and technology have enabled werewolves to blend easier and blend and mainstream with humans. It stated many even have normal jobs. The last chapter also described how to kill a werewolf by either stabbing it through the heart with any object or removing its head. She chuckled slightly to herself wondering, *how did these authors decide to write this as the two ways to kill a werewolf?* Francesca knew none of this was true, but she read the whole book while sitting at the table in the library.

Francesca thought of one evening in the 1840s when she helped a family of five escape a Georgia slave plantation. The father had been killed two days earlier for insubordination, and his wife and four children remained to serve their owner. Francesca had gathered blankets and clothing, stolen some bread from the owner's porch, tiptoed in before they fell asleep after crying together, and informed them she promised them freedom if they came with her.

She helped the family through the night, into the woods, up and down the North Georgia mountains, collecting water from the streams and springs. The mother carried the youngest baby, while the two other children tried their best to keep up. Francesca carried both older children in her arms much of the way. The family did not speak much as their shock remained from watching their husband and father hung from a tree two days prior.

After many days of hiding and sleeping in caves during daylight and long hikes at night, Francesca delivered the family to the Philadelphia Vigilance Committee. They had run out of food, they were tired and dirty, but they were free. Francesca knew they would never have their father to see them grow up and become free people, but as they sat at the library table, she assured the mother and children that he would be proud of them. The thought of that library table reminded Francesca where she is now and her task at hand.

She was about to leave when she remembered Patrick mentioning how vicious werewolves are in that they can often kill a vampire. She found this hard to believe because practically nothing or no one could kill a vampire. In fact, the few vampires she had ever known were all still walking the earth. She had never known a vampire to die. She decided to go into the vampire section and research vampires and see if werewolves were ever mentioned in those books. Again, the fictional books seemed more like comedies. There was however, one thick and dusty book that addressed vampires like they were real. She was surprised such a book existed. It appeared as if it had not been opened in decades. She flipped through the pages looking for any mention of a werewolf. The sound of the old and dried pages crinkled as she turned them. The smell was of old paper, old cigars, and wood stoves. When she finally reached chapter twenty-six, it was titled "How to Kill a Vampire." She tipped her head to the side as a puppy would do when questioning a command, he did not understand. She thought the author must have a lot of nerve to think there was an easy way to kill a vampire.

She turned the page and her pale skin crawled. There was a picture of a werewolf under a full moon attacking a vampire from behind. She slammed the book shut, sprang out of her chair, and gathered all her books. She was going to have to take this book home with her and read it cover to cover. She felt a new vulnerability she had never felt since Philip left that summer evening, as she headed home with her large and dusty book and turned down the sidewalk toward her house in Virginia Highland. Her thoughts were filled with questions and more questions. She needed to ask Patrick more about this. She wanted to know how he knew so much about them and what his experiences were with werewolves.

Within a few minutes she turned the corner onto her street and noticed Barry's car sitting in front of her house. As she drew nearer, she could see Barry's face and the big grin that crept across it when he noticed her approaching.

Chapter 15

Francesca leaned through the open window and kissed him on the cheek, holding the thick book behind her back. "I'm so glad you're here, come on in."

As Barry opened the door for her, she stepped in and dropped the book into a basket at the door. She quickly took off her sweater and draped it over the book. Barry closed the door seeing none of her actions.

"Where were you? I have been waiting quite a while. Did you forget our date?" Barry asked.

"Oh my God, I totally forgot. I went to the library and a couple bookstores and got so wrapped up in the books I lost track of time. I am so sorry. Can you forgive me?" Francesca asked.

"I suppose I can forgive you if you feel it in your heart to succumb to my wishes," Barry joked.

"And what wishes with those be?" Francesca quickly replied with a smirk.

"Uh, that you let me rub your feet and feed you grapes," he laughed.

"Good answer," Francesca replied, then burst out laughing. "Do you want to go somewhere? Have I ruined our evening? Would you like to stay and watch a movie?"

"Staying in and watching a movie actually sounds nice," Barry replied after looking in the distance in thought.

Francesca turned on the television, threw some popcorn in the microwave, poured Barry a glass of wine, and stepped into her room to change into her sexiest warm-ups, if such a thing existed.

She sat next to Barry, and the two enjoyed a movie while cuddled into each other's arms. She thought it funny how easily Barry could take her thoughts off bad guys and rapists. She reached in and took a handful of popcorn from the bowl in his lap. She decided to drink some wine with Barry, although she rarely ate or drank any human food, and had not actually had wine in fifty years.

When the movie finished, and the wine and popcorn were gone, Barry scooped Francesca into his arms and carried her to the bed. She had nearly fallen asleep during the movie. He kissed her on the forehead, covered her with the blankets, and was about to leave when she said, "Please stay." He turned back around, slipped off his clothes, and slid into bed next to her. Although she was very sleepy from the wine, she quickly pulled off her clothes and cuddled into him.

Lying behind her and kissing the back of her neck, he quickly had her on all fours and kissed her back from behind. She arched her back and moaned in delight. While holding her hair with one hand and cupping her breasts with the other hand he slowly entered. At first it was tender but progressed into deep and passionate thrusting. Francesca found herself moaning and gasping loudly as Barry continued to reach depths of her that no one had come close to. She thought of only Barry, and the world's troubles disappeared. His moans matched hers as their forceful thrusts climaxed into an explosive and shuddering symphony of cries of joy. They both collapse and exhaustion, with their sweat-tinged bodies draped over each other. Neither spoke but simply kissed each other and immediately fell into a deep sleep.

*****

Francesca dreamed of Philip running across the field with flowers in his hand for her. He was calling her name. He returned from France after changing his mind and not marrying the woman his parents had arranged. They met in the middle of the field laughing, playing, holding hands, and kissing. This dream, like all her other dreams, felt so real. She could hear his voice. She could feel his hair. She could smell his skin. These dreams made her feel like she was really with Philip. Philip was whispering to her, "Let us run Francesca. Let's run through the field together. Let's run. Let's run. Run. Run. Francesca run. He is a monster! Run," his voice echoed.

Francesca had been tossing during this dream and had awoken Barry. He had put his arm around her hoping to comfort her and calm her down. But when that did not work and she began to moan in her sleep, he opened his eyes to look at her. Her eyes were closed, and she was fast asleep, but in the moonlight her fangs shined bright for Barry to see. He did not flinch, he did not scare away, he simply continued to stare into her face.

Chapter 16

Ben was sitting home in his study with a stack of books of his own. His vampire books and weathered old journals were opened and laying on top of each other in disarray. He had scattered newspaper clippings of pit bull attacks throughout Atlanta. He was not reading any of them currently because he was dwelling on his mistake of letting Francesca see him at the funeral home. He was thankful he had worn the black coat and hat in case such an accident did happen. He did see her attempt to follow him as he snuck into a nearby alley, ran around back to the front of the building, and ducked out of sight until she stopped looking.

He turned back to his vampire books and continued to read them as if they were textbooks and he was studying for a research paper. He read the books throughout the evening and into the morning. He turned on the news and was happy to see no new attacks. Even though it was his day off, he knew the other medical examiners tended to save these cases for him. He had done most of them and they knew he showed more of an interest than they did.

Atlanta was bustling with activities and tourists today. The Braves game was starting this afternoon, art exhibits line the walkways of Centennial Park, the Georgia Aquarium was having its annual marathon, and the warm southern hospitality and weather drew many visitors. Ben opened his windows and doors to hear all the sounds of the people laughing, the birds chirping, the warm breeze blowing into his apartment. He walked over to the railing and looked at all the people below. He wondered if one of them could be Francesca. Now that he has seen her in person, he can watch for her.

Ben took great care to handle the books gently and not harm them with their delicate and dried bindings, as he picked up one of the old journals and began to read the cursive writing that filled the pages. He read the first page of the faded handwriting like he had read many times. "I have searched for her everywhere. Why did I take my eyes off her? I will continue to search until I find her. I can still smell her. I can still hear her voice."

Ben closed the book and decided he had read this passage enough times and headed out for a run in the park. Before he started his run, he stopped for an ice cream cone. In front of him was a lady with long red hair. His breath stopped as he thought it might be Francesca. He worked up the nerve to step around the side of her and purposefully bump her to create an opportunity to apologize and anonymously say hello. To his disappointment it was not her, but a high school girl who was there with her parents.

He walked on the sidewalks eating his mint chocolate chip cone, listened to a band playing in the distance, and watched the children play in the fountains that sprayed up underneath their feet intermittently. When he finished his cone, he licked his fingers and began his slow run. He ran down the tree-lined sidewalks, smelling the fresh Georgia air. He had to admit there was no air quite as sweet as North Georgia. In his years of searching, this was his favorite place. He ran past the waffle house, pass the Coca-Cola center, then turned early on Spring Street and headed north to avoid running near his work. He soon turned on 10th street and headed toward Piedmont Park. He enjoyed running most of his distance in the park and there was an art festival this weekend that he planned to see.

He reached the park and crossed through the stone gates and immediately saw thousands of people enjoying art, music, and food. City workers were setting up a stage and stands for a concert later tonight. He ran up the hills and turn the corners until he reached Lake Clara Meer. He turned to run the path along the lake and headed toward the botanical gardens where the trees and flowers smelled lovely and blew gently in the breeze. The children laughed as they steered their remote-control boats on the lake. He was beginning to feel winded when he passed through the dog park where the smell of flowers changed to a peculiar smell briefly. Ben thought nothing of it and never broke stride.

Ben looped around the botanical gardens and was heading toward Piedmont Avenue to make his turn and head back to home when he stopped in his tracks. He stopped so briskly that his lead foot made a loud thumping noise. Standing ten feet in front of him was Francesca buying flowers, and a crooked smile crept over his lips. *Had she seen him?*

Chapter 17

That evening, as Francesca talked like a little girl about her last few weeks with Barry, Patrick smiled and nodded as he dug through the bottom drawer of a large and old cabinet in the back corner. Francesca rambled on like a teenager-in-love and did not notice Patrick rummaging through the bottom looking for a specific wooden box. She was telling him about walks in the park with Barry, jokes he had told her, shopping together, stimulating conversations, when Patrick finally pulled out a hand carved wooden box holding it gently with both hands. Francesca stopped mid-sentence and asked, "What's that?"

"This my darling is for you," Patrick kindly said as he laid it on the table in front of her with his long, cold fingers. "I obtained this in 1744 on its way from Vienna to Switzerland, and it's all yours my darling. I never had a daughter and have never told you how proud I am that you put yourself through many years of college, you've managed to mainstream with humans on a daily basis, you're not afraid to stand up for what's right, and you're always kind."

Francesca lightly put her hands on the wooden box and began to open it. Her eyes shifted back to Patrick as she lightly said, "Don't forget, I'm also a cold-blooded carnivore. Thank you, what is it?"

"It's a 132-carat yellow diamond," Patrick said as Francesca lifted the box top by the hinges. The diamond sparkled in the candlelight. Francesca gasped at the beauty and the generosity of Patrick.

"I waited far too long to give this to you Francesca," Patrick said, "and seeing you so happy tonight makes me realize there's no better time than right now."

'How did you get it? It must have cost you a lot of money," Francesca replied.

"That's not important. The important thing is I have had it 270 years, and it's time that it belongs to you."

Francesca was speechless. She stared at the deep glow of the yellow diamond. She knew there was a large and colorful story behind this lovely gem, and she wondered if she would ever hear it. She stood slowly and hugged Patrick while kissing him on the cheek. "I'll never get married like a pathetic human, but if I did, I'd be honored if you'd walk me down the aisle."

Patrick held Francesca at arm's length by the shoulders and said, "I'd be honored to my dear." He kissed her on the forehead.

"Do you remember when I had to take you to the Republic of Hawaii in the 1800s to get you away from the Civil War and slavery? You were so wrapped up in rescuing the slaves that you would forget to eat for several days or even weeks." I was going to give you this gem before we left at that time, but you look so frail and weak, I forgot about it and just swept you out of here to the Pacific islands.

Francesca remembered the islands and their few years they spent there. She was thankful for Patrick rescuing her, as her time away made her realize she could not save all the slaves. They lived there at a time before the United States annexation and before the extreme overpopulation. She knew that trip had been hard for Patrick as he did not emerge into the general human population often, but she has convinced him to return a few times since then together. They both loved the islands over the decades, but watched them grow into an overcrowded, expensive, ghetto in many parts. Again, the bullying of the native people of the islands felt out of her control.

*****

Sergeant Franks had been working many long days and nights trying to solve these serial killer and serial rapist cases. *Were they related*? Just when he thought he was close to finding the attackers, he would come to a dead end. He had never been so frustrated with a case in his life. The latest rape victim had been discharged from the hospital and he just finished visiting her for the third time in which she refused to give any answers or testify in court. She simply said she did not see him at all because it was very dark and knew no one named 'Dave.'

Sergeant Franks kindly excused himself and said he would visit again soon, handing her his business card stating, "Call me if you change your mind or think of anything." The young lady simply nodded while looking into her lap, never raising her eyes to meet his. He called his crime lab one more time where he learned he did indeed have DNA results but no match in any system. This meant he does not have any DNA samples of the rapist and therefore could not identify him this way. Another dead end.

He thought he might consider retiring after this case, as he had been doing this several decades and it was not getting any easier. After his oldest daughter's recent death, and although his other children were grown lived in another state with his grandchildren, his wife had been asking him for several years to retire and travel. Maybe he would finally do it after this case was settled, to help his grieving wife. "First I will find you," he whispered toward the view out the window.

Chapter 18

The past two nights had been rather cool in North Georgia, as Francesca made her way through the parking deck up to the intensive care unit. As she stepped out of the elevators into the ICU, she could already hear Barry's voice saying, "Dr. Francesca will be here very soon." Apparently, a young married couple and the young wife's father had just bought a house in which electricity had not yet been activated. They were working on the cabinets and decided to bring in a kerosene heater to warm themselves in the cool night air. The father had been pronounced DOA while in the emergency room, the young husband was in the ICU in a coma with extreme carbon monoxide poisoning. His young wife was four months pregnant and was not affected enough to be admitted.

Although this young man, Brent, was in a coma and on life support, Francesca knew the only way he would survive was to get to the hyperbaric chambers two floors below. He would not survive without several of these treatments over the next few days. Francesca had treated several carbon monoxide poisoning cases and knew it was difficult to recover from such extreme poisoning, and hyperbaric chambers were the patient's best chance. Barry loaded up the portable ventilator, hooked all the intravenous fluids from his arm to the pole on the stretcher, and Barry, Brent, Francesca, and four other staff members headed to the elevator to descend to the hyperbaric chambers. Harry stayed a little late after his shift ended to help as well. Francesca was determined that this young boy was not going to die. He was not going to leave his young bride and unborn baby alone. She rolled Brent onto the hyperbaric bed with all his equipment, latched the secured doors, and started the high oxygen flow. At this point all Francesca could do was stare at the cardiac monitor hoping it would stay in a regular sinus rhythm, as he was locked in and unreachable. After eighteen minutes, Brent digressed to a heart rate of twelve. Francesca began yelling out orders. "Stop the chambers, we've got to get him out of there!"

Once Brent was out into the room, CPR was begun on this young man. Since he had such a young and healthy heart that could hopefully tolerate it, his dopamine infusion was opened wide up, because his blood pressure was 30/10. Within a few minutes Brent's heart rate and blood pressure return to normal, and there was no way Francesca could risk putting him in the hyperbaric chambers again unless he improved first. He had gotten little benefit from his eighteen minutes in the high oxygen flow chamber. The entire team and equipment returned to the ICU with no change in Brent's condition.

Barry brought Francesca a hot hazelnut latte as they sat and looked at each other, knowing they would probably lose this young man. Brent's pregnant wife was in the emergency room where her father's body remained. She had just called to check on Brent and Francesca told her of the events, lying to her when she said, "Maybe he'll be well enough to try again tomorrow."

She sipped on her latte and stared blankly at Barry as he did the same. Their only hope was that he was young and healthy enough to survive the night. This trauma victim did not have a bad guy that she could serve revenge upon, this unfortunate case was full of genuinely nice people trying to make a place to live. The father was helping his kids make the house their home.

The night shift dragged by slowly as Brent's vital signs roller coastered from near death to barely alive. When her shift finally ended, and her replacement arrived, Francesca told Barry to go home because she wanted to stay with Brent a little longer and help the day shift staff. She worked most of the day, finally met Brent's young and pregnant wife Melinda, and informed her he was not stable enough to try the hyperbaric chambers again today. She finally took it upon herself to go home, get some rest, and do it again tonight.

As she finally walked to her car, she was aware she was being watched. She often felt this because it was a large parking deck and several employees and family members sat in their cars for different reasons. She dismissed the feeling of eyes upon her and instead smelled the air. She dismissed the gentleman a few cars down in a long, dark coat. She was too tired to notice any people in their cars, any exhaust coming from their tailpipes, or the man watching her through binoculars. She simply backed out of her parking space and drove home.

Chapter 19

When she walked in her front door, her cell phone rang. It was Patrick. Francesca wondered why Patrick would be calling in the middle of the day as he was usually sound asleep or working on a funeral.

"Hi Patrick, what's up?" Francesca said with a tired happiness.

"A car has been sitting across the street from my funeral home all morning. There is someone in it and I feel like they've been watching me," Patrick said in a slight whisper.

"What does the car look like? What does the person in it look like?" Francesca said with a new alertness in her voice.

"It's a plain black sedan and I can't tell the make right now, and the windows are very tinted, I can just see a male figure. My staff is sick today, so I'm in the middle of a funeral and can't leave to go check it out," Patrick replied.

Francesca spun around on her heel, grabbed her sunscreen, headed right back out the door, got into her car and said, "I'll be there in five minutes."

When Francesca got about one-hundred feet from Patrick's funeral parlor, she saw the car he spoke of. She slowed down so she could get a better look without driving right up on him. Patrick was right, it was a black sedan and unmarked in any way. She could barely see a silhouette of a man through the dark windows, but she could hear his heart beating as it pounded faster with her approach. When she crept slower, the car sped off. "He's been there all morning, and he took off when I drove up? Really?"

Just then the funeral procession slowly drove out and blocked Francesca's chase of the black sedan. She tried to back up and head around the block to head off the car, but there were three cars stopped behind her. The funeral session appeared to drag on for twenty minutes. "He can be in Jacksonville by now!" She groaned.

She thought about going into check on Patrick, but knew he was in one of the front cars to go to the cemetery. After the last car of the procession slowly made its way out onto the street, Francesca followed only to turn the opposite way and head back home. Patrick answered his cell phone, "Did you see him?" Francesca stated she saw the car as a silhouette but could not get any identifying information including any smell. They talked a few minutes about how long the car had been there and that it could have been a family member of the deceased.

"Why would anyone want to watch you or follow you Patrick? You are the nicest man in this entire city. I think it was a family member who did not have the nerve to come into the funeral. I would not worry at all and I think you are fine. Have you spooked yourself with your werewolf stories?" Patrick agreed and stated he was just being overly cautious and was perhaps a bit tired himself. After thanking Francesca, Patrick informed her she should go home and get some rest. She knew she would have to find this man, and that he was probably not a family member of the deceased. She would keep a closer watch on Patrick.

Francesca immediately fell asleep, and dreamed of searching for Philip, unable to find him anywhere. She was on a ship to France to find him, and then suddenly she was in an airplane to France to find him, not only could she not find him, she could not seem to get to France. The dream kept taking her several places except France. She could not get to him. She could not find him.

Her dream quickly turned to her time in the Hawaiian Islands with the native drums beating on the beach. She ran into the water calling Philip's name and tried to swim to France to find him. The drums kept beating in the background as she tried harder and harder to swim but made less and less progress. She swam further only to find herself back on the shore closer to the beating drums. The natives danced on the beach and laughed at her. She turned to look at one man dancing and laughing who appeared to be Mr. Verone wearing his large hat.

She could hear Philip calling her name in the distance behind the drums. She stood to run to him, but her feet sank in the deep sand. The natives began to laugh more at her, and the drums began to beat louder and harder. She saw Patrick sitting on a rock whispering to her "He's watching you. He's following you."

Her dream quickly turned to pursuing the rapist. Again, she was looking for him and could not find him. She felt like she was close but was walking in slow motion and could never quite catch him. In her dream, she feared the werewolf, as she saw Patrick's face looking at her saying "Do not pursue this man. He is dangerous."

Then Patrick's face changed into Phillip's face and said, "He's a werewolf Francesca. Stay away. You do not know how to fight a werewolf. Runaway Francesca runaway."

As both Patrick and Phillip's images were chanting "Stay away from the rapist Francesca. Stay away from the werewolf Francesca." Francesca sat up in bed, panting, with her sharp fangs protruding.

Chapter 20

After another long night shift of taking care of Brent, who remained in a coma and who was still not well enough to go back to hyperbaric chambers, she went home. This routine went on for three days and three nights. Her thoughts were of Brent and his wife and unborn baby and pursuing the rapist. These thoughts tormented her, and she barely slept at all now. She thought maybe a different approach to the attacker might be better.

She now had four nights off in a row and stood on Peachtree Street looking at the medical examiner's building. Within minutes she was inside and meticulously reviewing each medical examiner's files. Ben's office was the third location of her search, when she found his name on the rapist reports. In fact, he had done *all* the reports. *Is this normal for one medical examiner to cover all the related cases? Was he covering his own tracks because he is the rapist?* she thought. She gasped as she also discovered he did all of her 'pit bull attacks' as well. She took cell phone photos of each report to decrease the time of her trespassing and improve the chance of her finding a clue to the rapist's identity.

When she finished the last report, she looked back at the medical examiner's name and wondered why it sounded familiar. *That name rings a bell*, she thought. She figured she must have heard on the news about all the attacks. She shut down the computers, closed all the files and drawers, and was about to head out when she saw a flash of a light under the door. She heard footsteps approaching as the light grew slightly brighter.

She was not sure what to do when an innocent person was about to discover her breaking and entering. She thought of hiding under the desk like a meager human. She looked around in a slight panic for a place to hide. She heard the doorknob rattle, saw it turn as the door slowly opened with a slight breeze. She could feel his approaching footsteps. She heard his heartbeat. The flashlight shined in, followed by a security guard, who smelled of a bacon diet and Mountain Dews. He shined it all around the room before completely entering and walking around the desk to the other side by the chairs. He walked over to the desk and shined it underneath, and behind the tall plants by the window, and stood for a few minutes in silence.

He turned back to the door, put his hand on the knob, and swept the flashlight around the room one more time. He then closed the door and assured it was locked. He slowly walked down the hallway and repeated this with the next eight rooms. He crept into the next room and looked under the desk and in all closets. Francesca could feel him drawing nearer to her new hiding spot at the end of the hall. How in the world could she get herself in such a predicament? She had not acted this amateurish in a long time.

The creaking of the floors drawing nearer to her made her realize the last time she was in this situation was in the slave quarters when the master came out to investigate a report of a woman wandering the grounds. He slowly went through each hut of each family, kicking in the doors, lifting the furniture, and throwing them across the room, searching for a strange woman. He had known of a woman that had visited other plantations and had killed their owners. He knew of the myth of a vampire stealing slaves.

The plantation owner slowly went from hut to hut, yelling at and questioning the servants, demanding they tell him her location. None of the slaves identified her or her location and many of them were beaten with his fist for their silence. As Francesca loomed in the rafters of the last hut, the owner entered. He could not see her dark figure up in the shadows, and when the slaves declined to have any knowledge of her existence, he beat the mother of the hut with his fist. She decided, on that night, she would never hide from men in the shadows again.

After the first strike on this innocent woman, Francesca almost invisibly descended upon him, opened her mouth big and wide with her fangs protruding, let him look into her glowing eyes, and bit down fiercely into his carotid artery. The slaves stood back against the wall in disbelief. Their eyes widened enough to take the whole violent scene in shock. No one screamed. No one said a word. They simply nodded a silent 'thank you' as Francesca dragged the body of the dead plantation owner into the woods and into the night.

Now Francesca stood in the parking lot watching the light flash from room to room. It had been a long time since she had to move at that speed to escape. She worried that the security guard had felt the wind of her movement as she ran past him, but he did not seem to feel or to see a thing of her fast vampire speed.

Once back in her home, Francesca began to read the reports, starting with the rapist reports. She read that these victims seemed to have dog bites throughout their bodies, various broken bones, large bruises everywhere, and always semen. There were always large amounts of blood at the scene and were pronounced DOA. She did know one survivor was not at the medical examiner's office and planned to question her after she had had time to recover. After reading all the rapist reports, she flipped to the pit-bull attack reports.

She read about the large bite marks that appeared to be from a pit bull. This was common knowledge on the nightly news. She felt her vampire heart skip a beat when at the bottom of each report was a small taped addendum stating, "unofficial and not divulged to the police department: patient was devoid of blood both at the scene and internally."

"Oh my God this man is aware and kept the lack of blood a secret. What else does he know? I drink too much blood at each of these scenes. Why would he keep this a secret from the police department and the press?" Francesca whispered and found herself pacing from room to room. How could she be so careless? How could she not think that a medical examiner would be aware of how much blood should be present in a dead victim? Just then it dawned on her as she looked at her phone; Dr. Ben Waters was the man who called that day, asking for her by name, and then hung up.

Chapter 21

Francesca did not sleep at all that night or day. She could not stop thinking about Dr. Ben Waters, and spent the entire night and day searching him on the Internet. She did not find much except where he went to school, where he graduated, and where he currently worked which was the exact place she broke into last night. Why was there no other information on this man?

Francesca called Patrick and discussed her entire night's activities and the reports she read. Patrick stated he had never heard of Dr. Ben Waters and said he would try to do a little searching of his own for her. She informed him of her phone call from the doctor weeks ago and that he had identified himself and asked for her by name and once she positively identified herself, he immediately hung up. She found that more alarming the more she learned about him.

She decided to stop researching and called the hospital to check on Brent. The charge nurse surprisingly put her through to Brent's table-side phone, and Brent answered the phone. His wife sat next to him. He had been extubated, and all his tubes and intravenous lines were stopped that morning. Brent even calculated how many days he had been there and how many days Francesca predicted he would remain until discharge. She was so proud he did simple math and that it looked as if he had no brain damage from his severe carbon monoxide poisoning. She informed him how proud she was, and Brent thanked her repeatedly.

"I will be in there tomorrow night to take care of you all night, and if you continue to do well you can probably discharge the next morning," Francesca informed Brent. She could hear him repeat that to his wife who audibly giggled in delight. Francesca continued to give her condolences for Brent's father-in-law. The two conversed in an intelligent conversation for the next ten minutes before Brent hung up and ate his first full meal.

As Francesca hung up a news bulletin flashed across her television screen. She turned the volume up. Apparently, the Atlanta police raided a sex trafficking gang, arrested two of the members, but four more had escaped before they could be caught. Sergeant Franks appeared on the screen stating, "If you see these gentlemen, please call 911 immediately and do not approach them, as we fear they are armed and extremely dangerous. They were here at the scene approximately four hours ago before escaping out a back door." Sergeant Franks went on to state they had found and rescued sixteen young girls from the age of six to sixteen. He did not comment any more on the girls' state except to say authorities were in the process of attempting to find these girls' parents.

Francesca rose from her seat. She now knew the sex traffickers at the scene could not have much of a head start, and she believed she could find them. She spent the rest of the day getting ready for her excursion. She got her prosthetic pit bull jaws, her dark clothing, drank one of the bags of blood that Patrick had given her, then took a shower to prepare for her hunt for the sex traffickers. Sergeant Franks had mentioned they did not know any of their names except one gentleman whose name was David Johnson: a twenty-four-year-old American male from Miami. "Hmmmm, that's Sally's boyfriend's name."

That was all the information Francesca needed at this point. She would focus on Dave tonight, and then focus on the remaining traffickers by scent and by name once the information was released. She knew Dave's scent. She clasped the black backpack containing her equipment, pulled her damp hair back in a ponytail, put on her black hat, and headed out the front door slamming it behind her. She enjoyed pursuits by foot because it gave her a chance to clear her head. She was a finely tuned killing machine but liked to think through her process before arriving, especially since nearly being caught at Dr. Waters office.

Dave was not difficult to find for Francesca. She went to the scene that Detective Franks had been reporting from, caught his scent, and followed it to a nearby rundown house near the airport. She was not sure which sex traffickers she was following due to the numerous scents, but also wondered if she might find all of them in one place even though police had not released the others' names. She lurked in a large tree high above the house for several hours waiting for someone to come out. When a large gentleman, who fit Sergeant Franks' description, walked out the back toward his car, Francesca jumped thirty feet below and landed right in front of him. She did not display her fangs just yet. She simply said, "Dave?"

The man's reflexive answer was "yes" before he could run away. He was more than a little startled by a woman appearing from nowhere in front of him.

She let him run only a few feet so as not to risk being seen by others. She wanted him to know why he was going to be brutally killed and she wanted him to suffer just as he has made many young girls suffer. He ran as fast as he could away from her, when suddenly she stood in front of him again. He turned and ran back from where he started, and she was there again in front of him. He stopped in shock and saw the fangs: shining, white, long, and sharp. That was the last thing he saw before they sank into his neck.

Francesca enjoyed drinking the blood from this despicable creature who bought and sold young girls for sex and slavery. She wanted to rip him apart but knew that is not how pit bulls attack. She was careful to not drink all the blood tonight and left much more than she had been in the past. She did this for Dr. Ben Waters' sake. After the man's body lay in a limp pile, she pulled out her prosthetic pit-bull jaws, clasped her fingers into the handles, and use them to bite into and over her vampire fang bite marks. She took out a large chunk of his neck as a pit bull would do. She threw the removed portion into her backpack, jumped back into the same tree, and in one leap over the neighbor's fence, and was gone without a sound. "Damn, he tastes good, but that was not Sally's boyfriend."

Her cheeks were always rosy after such a feast. She felt extra strong and fast after these attacks. "One down, three to go," she whispered to herself as she ran up Dogwood Drive back toward home in Virginia Highlands. She took note to smell for nearby pit-bull, found one in Hapeville, reached into her backpack, and threw the large portion of the sex trafficker's neck into the fence where the pit bull lived. "Enjoy buddy," is all she said as she never broke stride.

Chapter 22

The next evening, after she had completely discharged Brent from the hospital, and when he was home and recovering, she was feeling particularly good. She even invited Barry over after their shift ended. They talked about their patients, their activities for the last two days after not seeing each other at work, and Francesca told him a little about Patrick. Surprisingly, Francesca thought Barry still seemed a little jealous of her friendship with Patrick. She cannot put her finger on it, but he began to act a little standoffish. They sat on the back deck the remainder of the night, listening to the Georgia crickets, and watching the fireflies.

"So, are you going to spend your day tomorrow with Patrick?" Barry asked looking into the night.

"I had thought about it but haven't decided," Francesca answered simply.

"Why? Does he have more gifts for you?" Barry continued to avoid eye contact.

"Gift?" Francesca questioned, having made a point of not sharing the beautiful diamond Patrick had given her. Especially since she had suspected it was the diamond that was missing from a well-known jewel heist a few hundred years ago.

"Yes," he replied, "You briefly mentioned Patrick gave you something the other day and you would not elaborate what it was."

"Oh that! Oh, that was nothing. It was some old thing he had lying around," Francesca replied. She was telling the truth. She did not lie to Barry, but she could see he did not believe her. She had never seen a jealous side of Barry and it was not very flattering. She began to think Barry was just like all the other human men she had encountered in her life. Jealousy is such a ridiculous and petty human emotion. *Why would she think he was different? Why would she think she could be happy with the human? Why do men always have to be jealous of other men?* They both sat in silence with their thoughts because Francesca was far too advanced to have a petty and argumentative conversation with anyone, and Barry simply sat in the rocking chair stewing. He could see Francesca's attraction to him declining.

*****

Ben unzipped the body bag of his newest pit-bull attack victim. The victim's identity had been plastered all over the news. The special report headline read "sex trafficking escapee found brutally attacked and killed allegedly by a dog." He was quite surprised when he unzipped the bag and found blood covering the victim's clothes and body. The large and gaping bite to the neck did indeed resemble a pit bull jaw imprint. No bones were broken, no other bite marks were found throughout the rest of the body. He sent samples from under the victim's fingernails but knew as with all the other pit-bull attacks there would be no evidence of another person or dog.

He sent locks of hair to the lab, accompanied by fingernail clippings, clothes clippings, saliva, blood samples, nasal samples, and fecal samples. He had done this with every case and every case came back clean. *Why did this one still retain some blood in his body, on his body, and at the scene of the crime?*

After he finished the autopsy, he went back to his office, filed his report, telephoned the police department with his findings, and turned on the television in the break room while sipping on stale coffee. There were further developments on the attack of this sex trafficker. Due to the attack, police were led to the scene, and found the remainder of the sex traffickers hiding in that home. All were arrested and are currently in jail. No young girls were recovered at the home. Ben lifted his cup to his mouth as if he were drinking, but the cup was covering his smile. "Well look at that!" he whispered to himself.

As the sun began to set, Ben headed back to his apartment on his bicycle. He was cutting through the park, when he realized he was riding right up on Francesca strolling down the pathway. She was with a man and both seemed to be in deep conversation. He almost managed to ride past them without being noticed, but at the last second, Francesca looked up and directly into his eyes. He thought she had a look of recognition, *but how? Why would she recognize him anyway? She had never met him.*

Ben felt like he was getting a little too close. He thought maybe he should start giving these attacks to the other medical examiners. That was what he would do. He would begin to see less complicated cases. He needed to step back. Francesca looked at him with acknowledgement in her eyes. His mind was spinning. He looked back after passing to assure he had really seen her, and she kept walking without breaking stride or looking back at him. *Did he imagine she recognized him? Surely, she did not know who he was.* He tried to convince himself.

He decided instead of going straight home, he would treat himself to The Varsity to calm his nerves, but thought he needed to finally stop in as he had passed it every day. With his to-go bag in hand, he made his way back to his apartment. With a giant Coke, and a bag of food in one hand, and his keys in the other, he fumbled but finally opened his front door. He tossed the bag on the table and sat the large Coke next to it while dropping his keys onto the counter and turning to switch on the light. Instead he saw a dark figure sitting in his chair in the living room. He gasped, switched the light on with one hand, while grabbing a chair and holding it up like a matador.

With her arms spread out across the back of the couch and her legs crossed, Francesca solemnly said, "Hello Ben."

Chapter 23

"Who are you? What are you doing here?" Ben sputtered out while now holding the chair with both hands and rocking back and forth on his feet.

"Really Ben? You're defending yourself against me with a chair?" Francesca said without moving.

Ben looked down and realized he was holding his dining room furniture up like a sword. "Oh," was all he said as he put it back in its place while shaking in fear. Francesca calmly asked, "Why so nervous Ben? Were you nervous when you called me on the telephone? Were you nervous when you were stalking my friend Patrick? Were you nervous when you are following me in the park today?"

"What?" was the only word Ben could muster. Francesca decided she would not say any more to him and just enjoy watching him squirm. She watched him open his mouth several times and attempt to speak but nothing would come out. He did not take his eyes off her, but he reached back with his left-hand fumbling until he found the chair he was just holding and stammered back to sit in it.

"Why would a man in his own apartment, and as tall and muscular as you, be afraid of a small female like me? What is it about me that scares you? Aside from your little chair made of toothpicks, you have not reached for a gun or knife or any other items to defend yourself against an intruder," Francesca continued to speak without moving. "Why don't I know much about you, yet you seem to know an awful lot about me? Let us get to the bottom of this." She clicked fingernails on a pile of books in her lap that Ben had not noticed until now. He quickly jolted his gaze to the coffee table which was now void of all his books.

When Ben continued to sit in a seemingly paralyzed state, she quickly rose to her feet scattering books everywhere, and was suddenly eye-to-eye, nose-to-nose with Ben. Being careful not to expose any fangs, Francesca gutturally growled, "I said, who are you?"

Ben managed to eke out, "I'm Dr. Waters. I'm a medical examiner." He knew to not move an inch and just answer the questions.

"I mean who are you really?" Francesca roared. "Are you a rapist? Am I your next intended victim? Have you been examining all of your own attacks all this time to cover your own tracks?" She nearly asked him if he is a werewolf but feared she would give away her own identity with such a question. "Did you rape and kill those women?"

"What? Me? No! I have never hurt anyone in my life. I think I should call the police now," Ben finally began to speak. "Obviously, you're no good-guy, what with breaking and entering in everything." His speech was hurried in an octave higher than normal. "Why in the world would you break into my home and question me? I have not been following you and who's Patrick?"

Francesca continued to stare into his eyes evaluating his genuineness. She slowly stretched her arm out and grasped Ben's soda. "You look like you need a drink of this." Ben turned his gaze to look at his soda which was now perspiring on the outside. With a shaking hand, he reached out to take it and slowly turned his gaze back to Francesca who was gone! He quickly scanned the room, stood, and looked behind him. She was nowhere. He slowly rested the soda back onto the table with his unsteady hand. His whole body shook now.

After several minutes, Ben smiled slightly and whispered to himself, "You'd be so proud of me. You've described how beautiful she is but not nearly as beautiful as the real person." He knelt and slowly picked up all the books that were scattered throughout the room by Francesca. Bookmarks had been thrown out and laid randomly throughout the room. Some books laid facedown while others piled on top of each other. What had she read? What did she know? She obviously wanted me to know she had read them. Why didn't she ask about the contents of the books? He slowly straightened each book meticulously and stacked them up neatly on the table before grabbing his bag of food and plopping deep into the couch. "Woo hoo!" Loudly escaped his lips like a college boy at a Falcons game.

Francesca slowly walked up Ponce de Leon Place toward home as she contemplated her short and sweet conversation with Ben Waters. He had sounded way too sincere to be the rapist, but he had to be. She had never met a werewolf, so she was unsure of how to evaluate the fact that he did not seem like one. *What does a werewolf seem like? What does a rapist seem like?* She supposed being kind and sincere must be part of the mode of operation for a werewolf or rapist. *Isn't that how they lure their prey? Isn't there kindness what their victims fall for?* Her suspicions began to grow all over again.

She was so deep in thought about her encounter with Dr. Ben Waters that she did not notice one man following her in the crowd of people on the streets. He stayed way behind so as not to be noticed. He knew being caught by a creature such as Francesca would be fatal. He knew she would detect his scent if he got any closer. He knew to stay far behind, and he knew where she was going. He has been watching her. He knew where she works, where she lives, her friends, where her friends live, that she had to wear sunscreen to be out in the daylight, and he knew what she was.

Chapter 24

Philip rang the bell on Francesca's door. She had been far down in her lower basement cleaning and shining her prosthetic pit bull jaws. She was just putting them back into their velvet lined case when she heard the doorbell. She latched the wooden cases, and slowly ascended to her ground-level home. "Philip?" Francesca said surprisingly happy. "How did you get here? Why are you here? Where have you been? I've been looking everywhere for you."

Philip did not say anything. He simply grabbed Francesca in his arms and gave her a kiss that only Philip could give. She stopped talking and kissed Philip back as she went limp in his arms. He held her up, whispered in her ear, "I love you," then he casually walked into her kitchen. "I'm starving Francesca. I came extremely far to find you. Do you eat food? Or do you just pretend to eat food to keep up the façade?" He reached into the refrigerator pulled out an apple. He bit into it and kept talking with a mouth full of apple. "The coffee maker over there… You do not drink coffee. In fact, this whole kitchen is a waste of space. What is up with food? Why do you go on pretending? They all know."

"They all know what?" Francesca asked. She closed refrigerator behind him with a puzzled look on her face. Why was he here after all this time? Why did he suddenly show up? If he had been around all this time, why had not he let her find him. "I eat," Francesca simply replied, as she walked around the kitchen noticing all the items he mentioned.

"No, you don't Francesca," Philip calmly replied. "You regurgitate the food after no one is looking. The only thing you can safely consume is blood. You will not even lower yourself to drink the synthetic blood. You are too good for that. You drink blood from the dead. You drink blood from the people you kill. You are a killer. Did you ever wonder if you have killed innocent people? You're so high and mighty and righteous killing all the bad guys, did you ever stop and think maybe you're wrong and maybe you've been killing innocent people as well?" Philip lifted the lid off her cute cookie jar shaped like a penguin with an Atlanta Braves hat on top and pulled out a fresh cookie baked at a local bakery in Buckhead.

He bit into the cookie and stared at her face saying, "Don't you have anything to say for yourself? You are the judge and jury and you carry out the sentences? You are so sure you will never be caught? You think so lowly of these humans that you do not even care. You think they are food at your taking." Philip paced around the kitchen.

The only words Francesca could mutter were, "Where have you been? I've been looking for 200 years." She ran across the room to hug him but seemed to be in slow motion. The more she ran the slower she got and the further away he appeared. "Why did you leave me so long ago? Don't you know this happened to me because you left me? Don't you realize I would trade all this to be human again if I could be with you? My life has been so hard and long since you left. I had to leave my parents and my sisters behind."

"I had to live in caves and in the cold darkness eating rats for a long time when you left me. All I wanted was for you to come back, but I was so ashamed of what I had become. You are still a strong and handsome man, and I am this monster you see now. Why have you come back now? Why are you finally here after all this time?"

"He's coming for you, you know. You have been made. Your identity has been hacked. They know you and they know who you are. You got clumsy. You got careless. You have been discovered. They are going to kill you. They are going to kill you. They're going to kill you." These words kept repeating as they faded into the distance.

Francesca sat straight up in bed with her fangs protruding. Her dreams were becoming more vivid and more disturbing. This dream felt like he was here in the house. She could hear his voice like he was lying in the bed next to her. She could smell his sweet smell still. She laid back down as she grabbed the extra pillow and hugged it to her chest. She retracted her fangs. *Why couldn't she stop dreaming about Philip? Why were her recent dreams so disturbing?*

She thought just then, her most recent dreams had been a warning from Philip. *He had been trying to warn her in her dreams. Of course, that's ridiculous, Philip has been gone a long time, and these are warnings from my own subconscious. Why do they have to come in the form of Philip? Why do they have to haunt me throughout my days and nights? What is it I see by myself that I need to be aware of?* Just then something brushed against her leg under the covers.

Chapter 25

She heard a sigh, looked over and realized Barry had been sleeping beside her the entire time. He had not flinched. Thank God he could not read her thoughts. She rolled over on her side, wrapped her arm around Barry's chest, and began playing with the curly hairs. He moaned and held her hand on his chest. She kissed the back of his neck and closed her eyes to go back to sleep. Barry had other plans.

He slowly rolled her over, kissing every inch of her body, until she moaned in delight. Neither spoke a word, as Barry continued to kiss her toes, working up her legs until she cried out in delight. Strong arms lifted her onto her hands and knees once again, as he pounded her with strength and passion from behind. She never felt such vitality and had to hold on to the headboard for support. He might be a meager and jealous human, but the sex was incredible.

Both collapsed into an exhausted pile together while their breathing slowly returned to normal. Barry immediately fell back to sleep. Although Francesca wanted to do the same, she did not want to have another dream about Philip. She lay there thinking about a conversation with Ben, and almost laughed out loud remembering the frightened look on his face. She could barely hear her own thoughts as Barry snoring grew louder and louder.

She started to uncover herself to get up and head to the shower when Barry stopped snoring and jolted out of bed himself. "I've got to go. I'm late to an appointment." He threw on his pants and shirt.

"What appointment? Where are you going? Stay here and cuddle with me," Francesca pretended to be interested in his human emotions.

"I've just got a thing at a place," Barry answered evasively as he threw on his shoes, and as Francesca rolled her eyes.

"Okay bye," Francesca said while throwing an imaginary kiss his way. Barry did not even see the gesture because he was already halfway out the front door. As it slammed behind him, Francesca slowly got up and headed to the shower. They must have spent more time in bed than she thought because the sun had already set. "Geez humans."

Dressed in blue jeans and a tank top, Francesca decided to have a pint of blood, and read some more of her books. Although they were obviously fictional, she wondered if she could pull more truths out of the fabrications. The book stated werewolves were first known in the year 1100. Francesca realized that was at least when the myths were created. She remembered Patrick had said there are only two ways to kill a werewolf. The first was with silver bullets, just as mentioned in these books, but Patrick said it often takes five to ten bullets to kill a large werewolf.

She had forgotten the Patrick mentioned the other way to kill the werewolf was with an angle blade. *What in the hell is an angle blade*? She looked through the books to find angle blades mentioned and could find nothing. She finally googled what an angle blade looks like and was shocked to see the images, as Patrick has several of these displayed on his walls. They have long silver handles with a long sharp blade similar to an oversized ice pick. She thought she might have to visit Patrick tonight and ask about these blades. He had never really elaborated about how he got them or where they came from.

She continued to read for the next several hours about how werewolves can blend in with humans more easily than vampires. The book stated very few vampires try or successfully blend or 'mainstream' with humans and that it was far more common to find a werewolf mingling in society. She thought about Dr. Hepner, who worked in internal medicine, and how if anyone were a werewolf it would be him. His chest hair protruded up through the top of his shirt, and you could see back hair rippling the back of his shirt. He had very thick eyebrows and a lot of facial hair that he unsuccessfully attempted to keep clean shaven. She laughed to herself.

She suddenly looked at the time on her phone, jumped up, texted Patrick that she was on her way to visit. She knew he would have a warmed glass of blood waiting for her, with his nice piano music playing in the background. He knew she loved this, and it was always a special night for both. She threw her damp hair in a ponytail and darted out the door.

Chapter 26

Within minutes she arrived at Patrick's front door and let herself in with her key. The formal funeral parlor was empty and dark which meant Patrick had already retired for the evening and was downstairs. She made her usual way back to the secret entrance but found the door open. "Patrick?" she inquired, knowing he must be nearby because he would never leave this secret door open and risk being discovered by humans. When there was no answer, she repeated it several times, looking around the room. She detected an unusual smell.

She slowly descended to his living quarters far below and repeated his name, "Patrick?" There was still no answer. She was relieved when she could hear him moving around in the rear room. He must have been busy because he always greeted her when she arrived. "Patrick. Oh Patrick," she announced playfully. There was still no answer. She detected an unusual scent again only much stronger down here. She figured Patrick must have guests, but she never remembered him having anyone besides her in his lower quarters. She continued to walk slowly toward the noise she had heard which had since grown very silent.

As she entered Patrick's living quarters, she stepped into a room of chaos. All of Patrick's belongings were scattered on the floor desks and chairs. Most of his antique items were pulled from the walls. His desk was turned over. There were large holes dented into the walls. "Patrick, where are you?" Francesca yelled, with fangs protruding. Still no answer. She lifted her nose and smelled the air as the scent began to upset her nares.

She made her way around the overturned desk and gasped from deep within. There on the floor laid the remains of Patrick, or at least what she assumed was Patrick. She had never seen a dead vampire before. She had heard the stories of how they had converted into bloody and gelatinous liquid but had never imagined it would be this large amount or that it would be her dear old friend Patrick.

Before she could react, she heard the same noise from another room. She realized now it was a creaking floorboard. Patrick's killer was here. He would not be for long, because she would rip him apart. Even her fangs appeared slightly longer and sharper than usual. In a flash too fast for the human eye, she was in the other room. There was no sign of this murderer. She ripped open the closet doors, ripped open the cupboard doors, flip the bed upside down, she went room to room destroying Patrick's home even further while she searched for this killer.

She did not have time to be upset over Patrick's violent death, at least not yet. She searched and sniffed the air as she moved rapidly throughout Patrick's home. She continued to search for nearly another hour and to smell this scent, but the death of her dear old friend began to sink in. She returned to where his remains laid in a puddle on the floor. In the middle of the pile, she noticed a glimmer of light reflecting off something shiny. She reached down and picked it up. It was one of Patrick's angle blades that had hung displayed on the wall. He must have been holding this during the attack.

She sat on the corner of the turned over desk and waited for this creature to appear. She decided since she had looked everywhere, she would lure him to her. He had no idea of her rage or her strength. She waited patiently with the angle blade tucked in her rear belt loop. She knew it was a matter of time before he showed himself. If she had to die to defend Patrick's honor, she was willing, but the adrenaline that shot through her veins with her anger was stronger than anything willing to attack her or Patrick.

She sat in the complete darkness listening to the creaks of the floorboards, smelling the scent of her next kill, waiting. Flashes of her life with Patrick appeared in her mind. She remembered how he had helped her become a vampire who could come out of the shadows and caves of hiding. She remembered that Patrick had found her hiding in an old abandoned well in the middle of the night in Louisiana. She remembered how he took months to gain her trust to speak to anyone at all. She remembered him bringing her to Atlanta when she was weak and frail because she refused to drink from a human. Nearly two hundred years of her friendship with Patrick unfolded in her mind.

She recalled the time he showed her a drawing of his wife and three children taken soon before he was turned to a vampire himself. The two of them had visited his family's gravesite from time to time in Louisiana. She hoped they were together again, and that if there really was a hell Patrick did not deserve to go there.

Chapter 27

The creaks in the floor were not where the attacker came from. He was right behind her hiding in the closet next to Patrick. His odor was so strong that it filled the room and was difficult for her to detect its origin. She spun around just in time to see a large mouthful of long and sharp teeth sink into her neck, then her shoulder, then her rib cage. She had never been caught off guard and was truly bewildered. She slung the blade around trying to land it into the heart of this creature's seven-foot-tall frame, but as he continued to bite her, she kept missing.

She managed to break free from him and threw him across the room. "My God!" He was massive and long hair covered his whole body, and his long snout housed a full mouth of long sharp jagged teeth. Dried blood covered his nose and chin. She knew some of this was hers but most of it was Patrick's. He stood like a human but had feet, paws, and claws of a wolf. He had a part of a torn shirt still over one arm and shoulder and hanging down his back. It was as if he had grown out of his clothes and this was all that had not ripped off.

She attacked him again with her knife leaning it in his rib cage but missing his heart. He jolted away before she could pull the knife back out, and the handle protruded out of his chest while he pounced on her again. He picked her torso up with his jaws and flung her across the room leaving jagged fang marks on her rib cage and back. She lay in a limp pile for second, then sprung to her feet and faster than the werewolf's eyes could see, and she bit into his neck while wrapping her legs around his trunk. He howled and whimpered and threw her to the floor like a rag doll.

He stood over her and stared down at her while reaching his right hand to his left chest and gently pulled the knife out of his rib cage. It did not seem to faze him at all. He held the blade up with both hands as he planned to lunge it into Francesca's heart. He brought the knife down to the floor and a loud bang; she was no longer there. The creature spun around to see her as she attacked him and ripped the remnants of his remaining clothes off and bit into the back of his neck. Again, he howled and then fell to the floor in pain.

The werewolf stammered to get back up when Francesca bit him in the neck again. He was too strong for her to drink any of his blood to weaken him. He would throw her off before she could take his life. His skin was thick and hot, and his hair was wiry and course. He got up and was about to lunge at her again when he noticed her gaping bite wounds healing before his eyes. He cocked his head to the side like a confused dog.

For the first time, Francesca's small frame was a disadvantage against this giant werewolf. She lunged at him with her strong and powerful vampire strength as he also lunged at her with his seven-foot-tall monstrous and muscular body. He knocked her to the floor, and she rolled through the bloody goo of Patrick. Now covered and dripping in Patrick's remains, she felt weak and defeated. She was tired. They fought for two more hours, destroying Patrick's home even further. Just when Francesca would heal and get her strength back, the werewolf would rip into her again.

This werewolf did not seem to be tired at all. *Was this Ben? Had she made him mad during her visit? Had he followed her there? Why would he kill Patrick and not her? Why didn't he just kill her when she was in his apartment?* These thoughts ran through her head as she laid in a pool of remains and broken furniture. She slowly stood again, with great effort, and stammered and wobbled while holding onto the side of the broken desk. "Ben, you're going to die," she whispered. Again, the werewolf cocked his head to the side with confusion.

She continued to regain her strength only to lose it again for nearly two more hours of fighting with this giant creature. For the first time, she wondered if she would survive. Visions of Philip now filled her head. She could hear his voice calling her name. She could see him running through the meadow with her. He was standing on her front porch with a bouquet of wildflowers tied with a simple string. A lock of hair fell into his eyes as he smiled at her. She could hear him sing to her, "Fight Francesca fight. Fight. Fight. He is here to fight for you. He is here to protect you. He is here. He's here."

Her eyes were closing as she heard Phillips comforting voice, but before they closed completely, the werewolf arched his back and cried out in pain as he was lowering the knife toward her. He then stood still looking down on her, before he slowly fell to the floor like a large tree. Part of his large torso fell on her and she quickly rolled him off. His stench was nauseating. She looked up and behind where the werewolf had stood was Ben. He held the angle blade in his hand that he had just pierced through the werewolf's heart.

They looked at each other momentarily for both were in a slight state of shock. Finally, bending down he asked "Are you okay Francesca? How badly are you hurt?" Francesca, still confused, looked over at the werewolf. He was no longer moving or breathing. She rolled on her side to meet eye to eye with the dead werewolf. He stared at her even in death. She looked back at Ben then at the werewolf then back at Ben trying to make sense of everything. She then noticed the werewolf's wrist had a glisten of something shiny catching her eye. It was a watch that must have stayed on when he turned into this hideous werewolf.

Ben lifted her and took her to the next room away from Patrick's remains and the dead werewolf. The two sat silently for several minutes while she caught her breath and tried to get over the shock of their evening. "I thought you were the werewolf,"

Francesca finally whispered. "I thought you were the person raping and killing all those women. I thought you were the one who was going to try to kill me."

"I would never harm you Francesca," Ben said with sincerity. "I have been keeping an eye on you, but it is not to harm you. Besides, I could not even if I wanted to. You are smoking hot, vampire, and I am a measly human man." Just when Ben was about to explain who he really was, they both turned to listen to the sound from the room they had just left. Ben grabbed the blade to protect Francesca as they ran back into the room with the bodies. There was no werewolf. He was gone.

Chapter 28

As Ben methodically searched the entire lower level of Patrick's home, Francesca stealthily searched all the other levels and outside for the werewolf. They both returned to the pile of remains of Patrick empty-handed. The werewolf was gone, and neither were sure they could kill him.

Ben volunteered to help clean up what remained of Patrick as well as straighten all the damage from the hours of fighting. Francesca quietly answered, "Thank you but this is something I need to do myself. Patrick would do it for me. You go home and get some sleep. Thank you, Ben, for being there for me; I thank you for saving my life." She proceeded to scoop up the gelatinous and dark red remains of Patrick in an old container he had on the shelf since she knew him. She thought it was appropriate, as she remembered he told her it was an urn he had obtained in Egypt many centuries ago. She thought he would approve of such a final resting place.

She worked through the daylight hours putting Patrick's home back together as best she could. She knew he had always taken great pride in his home and rarely left it except to pick up a body at the hospital or attend a funeral home service at the cemetery. She knew where almost every piece of his antique furniture was obtained, and the story behind it. She piled the broken furniture pieces as best she could to repair on another day. Patrick's remains were placed on the shelf and lying beside his werewolf-killing blades.

He had tried to warn her and protect her from the werewolves, and in the end, it was his demise at the hand of such a creature. Patrick was her only true friend. He had raised her from a young vampire. He had saved her when she was too scared to eat humans and was weak from anorexia. He was a father to her, a best friend, a confidant, and a true gentleman. He tried to warn her that someone was watching him, and she put little effort in the validity of his fear.

As the sun set and the moon rose, Francesca drove home. She stood at her front door in the darkness reluctant to go in. Somehow her own home felt emptier than it ever had now that Patrick was gone. She looked over at Sally's empty house, which still had police tape around the porch columns. She decided to take a long deep breath to see if she could smell any familiar or odd smells. Now that she knew what the werewolf smells like, surely it would be easier to find him.

******

Ben laid on his couch with his television on, which he was not watching. He simply stared at the ceiling trying to process his recent events. He had moved here expecting drama, but he never imagined what he just experienced. The news was on the television, and after lying motionless for one hour, he realized there was no mention of a rapist tonight. He realized the Atlanta news did not report as much violence as usual. *Oh, they would have a heyday with this story,* but he would not think of a way to call it in without sounding crazy or exposing Francesca. It suddenly made sense that the werewolf was indeed the rapist. It fit all his autopsies.

As he began to relax and breathe a sigh of relief, he heard a creak come from his bedroom. He quickly sat up and reached for the blade he held earlier, but he had left it at Patrick's home. He stood and crept toward the bedroom when the werewolf appeared in the doorway. The werewolf stared straight at Ben, tilted his head as any dog does, and with saliva dripping from his fangs, slowly walked toward Ben.

"You came to finish me off, huh? Well come and get me. Get it over with, but you are no match for Francesca, and now that she is on to you, she will kill you. You may have had the element of surprise once, but that is gone now. After you kill me, she will eat you for dinner."

The werewolf simply kept walking toward Ben slowly. Without turning his head, Ben reached down and felt for anything on the coffee table he could get his hands on. He wrapped his fingers around something and quickly swung the remote control like a machete toward the werewolf.

The werewolf swung his left arm backhanded toward Ben which threw him across the room and against the wall, and his ribs audibly cracked. He slumped to the floor in pain gasping for his breath. He looked up at the towering werewolf and said, "Come on, finish it." The werewolf flung him back to the other side of his apartment and onto the kitchen counter, flinging the coffee maker onto the floor and shattering the dishes on the rack. Ben's arm twisted under him as he lay unable to move.

The werewolf slowly walked toward Ben when the front door flew open, and a flash of light streaked across his vision. Ben could only lay there on his side, shoved toward the back of the kitchen counter, watching as Francesca clung onto the back of the werewolf with her fangs longer and sharper than ever, plunging into his neck. The werewolf cried out in pain and flung her off and onto the floor. She laid there looking up at him with her red and glowing eyes.

The werewolf jumped into the air and came upon her with all four paws extended. Again, the only sound to be heard was that of a crying wolf in the night. The werewolf fell limp and lifeless as Francesca shoved Patrick's blade through his heart. He let out one final whimper before Francesca rolled his lifeless body off her. She stood, while Ben lay holding his ribcage with his one unbroken arm and watched the werewolf for fear, he was still not dead.

After several minutes, the werewolves body began to creak, grind, and shrink back into its human form. Ben managed to get himself off the kitchen counter, onto the floor and limped over to Francesca and the transforming body on the floor. "Barry, Barry, Barry, you naughty boy," was all Francesca said as she looked at the watch with a big red secondhand on Barry's wrist. She had seen the secondhand when he lay on the floor Patrick's funeral home. She knew Barry was going to follow Ben to kill him.

Epilogue

Ben and Francesca sat on the floor together staring at a dead Barry. Neither spoke for quite a while as Francesca simply stared, and Ben wrapped his arms around his rib cage in pain. "Do you mind telling me now who you really are?" Francesca said to Ben without taking her eyes off Barry. Ben took a heavy sigh and kept his eyes on Barry as he began to explain.

"I inherited my great grandfather's times ten generation's diary. It has been handed down for generations and has been kept in a protective case. When I was a little boy, my grandfather decided to open the case and read it before he died. It told of a man who moved from France to America when his wife had died and his children had grown. It had long details and many dates searching for his one true love. It stated he had never loved anyone but her. He looked everywhere for her in Louisiana and surrounding areas," Ben calmly began despite his painful ribs.

Ben continued, "The diary displayed a true broken heart and a man longing for his love that he had abandoned. He searched for many, many years and followed clues and rumors of her locations and where she might have moved to. He spent the rest of his life looking for her. He wrote of the rumors that she had been turned to a 'woman of the night 'also known as a vampire."

Ben continued, "He searched for her until the day he died. He never remarried, he never gave up looking for her, and he died a broken man. My great, great times ten grandfather's name was Philip. After my father and grandfather read this diary with me, I decided to take up the search in my great-great grandfather's place. When I heard of mysterious deaths that resembled attacks of pit bulls in Atlanta, I thought it could be a vampire and hopefully be you."

Ben took a minute to gather his thoughts and whimpered a little in pain as he cupped his ribs with his hands. Francesca was now looking straight at Ben with wide eyes in disbelief. "You are Philip's grandson? You have been searching for me? That diary on your coffee table was written by Philip himself?"

"Yes Francesca Philips, I found you. I found the fantastic, young, and beautiful redhead whose description fills the pages of several generations of my great-great-grandfather's journal. He searched for you, and he loved you until his dying breath."

The shrieks of an ambulance drawing near grew louder, as Francesca held Ben in her arms to comfort him, and she allowed tears of sadness and joy to flow down her cheeks for the first time in two-hundred years.

About the Author:

I See You is Pamela Roland's first novel. Pamela has been in the medical profession since 1980, beginning in the U.S. military, and now a medical provider herself. She has won several creative writing awards, has played in symphonies, and played professional volleyball. She has volunteered for several missions, community needs, and donates part of her proceeds to an elephant foundation in Africa.

AuthorPamelaRoland@gmail.com

Book 2 "I Hear You" in 2024

Book 3 "I Feel You" coming soon